Fallin' In Love With The Goat 3

By: Tiece

Text Tiece to 42828 to sign up for
Email Alerts

By: Tiece

Recap

"Bestie, they really did the damn thing this year." Cashmere said, as she sipped from her cranberry juice."

Shyla nodded her head to agree. "Yea, it's really pretty in here with all the lights, the red carpet, the enormous buffet—"

"And, don't forget all these people dressed like they're attending an after party at the Oscars. Makes me wanna go shopping."

"The whole crew is wearing tailored suits and every last one of 'em has a pair of Louboutin Red Bottoms on their feet. I must admit, you and Justin look so good dressed in the same baby blue colors. Y'all look sophisticated and bougie at the same damn time."

Shyla grinned. "We do look good together. I never realized how handsome he was."

"That's because you never looked at any man but Rich."

"With his disrespectful, stupid ass." Shyla uttered. "But, Justin look so good tonight I'm thinking about giving him some."

"I'm surprised you haven't did it yet."

"He's the one that don't wanna go there. He knows the situation with Rich and he ain't with the games. Period," she added. "So, he's been making sure that I'm completely over it before he takes it there."

By: Tiece

"Well, he must really like you to do that. Most nigga's won't care if you're married, as long as you're giving up the goods that's all they want."

"Apparently, sex ain't all he wants."

"Do you want more, because it seems like it can go that way if y'all ever hook up?"

"Hell yea, I want more, and I'd love to have it with him." Shyla admitted.

"Aww, I like that." Cashmere said, just as she looked up to see Jabari and Tiana talking. "See, that's what I'm tripping about." She said with a frown on her face. "It's bad enough that he walked her in, but damn can he get out of her face already?"

"Chill out Bestie." Shyla told her. "This is definitely not the event to act a fool."

"I'm good. I'm just gonna sit back and play my cards right. I ain't giving her or him the time or day to take me out of character."

"Good," Shyla said, just as Justin walked back over.

"May I have this dance?" he asked Shyla. "You don't mind do you, Cashmere?"

"No, by all means sweep this pretty lady off her feet. She deserves it." Cashmere responded with a smile.

"I'll be back." Shyla said with a big smile on her face.

Cashmere sat at the table alone, as she took in the beauty of the party. Gold, white and black balloons were everywhere giving her the Hollywood themed feeling. It was gorgeous and the pictures of Skylar all about the place was definitely a reminder of how one should really enjoy life because for some it could be cut short in so little time.

"Hey," a light voice spoke, as the woman seemed to have snuck up on her.

"Hey," Cashmere spoke back with a nervous expression on her face.

"You look good tonight." Tiny said.

"Thanks, so do you." Cashmere responded.

"Well, I just wanted to come over and speak."

Cashmere turned on her fake smile. "Oh ok, nice seeing you again."

"Yea, same here." Tiny said, as she walked off.

The conversation was so brief that it frightened Cashmere, as she nervously sipped her drink. Tiny popping up on her like that scared the shit out of her. She didn't know what the girl had up her sleeves, but she was hoping that she'd mind her own business and stay the hell out of hers.

After scoping the scene once again, she noticed Jabari was nowhere in sight, but that Tiana and Lauren was now seated at a table about to eat. There were so many people in the building it was hard to keep up, but she had to keep Jabari in sight just so she'd know what he was up to at all times. "Where the hell is he?" she mumbled.

By: Tiece

"Hey nephew," Jabari said to Cannon, as he reached for him. "You look good as hell tonight." He told Yolanda, as she smiled while handing Cannon over to him.

"Thank you. You look very handsome tonight as well." She told him.

"I didn't know you were going to be here."

"Are you serious? I had to come because I'll be the one leaving with Cannon in about an hour. You know how my sister is. She loves to party and I'm always the babysitter."

"Dang, I feel you though. I appreciate you showing my nephew so much love and attention."

"Well, he is my nephew too." She teased.

"You're right," Jabari said, just as his conversation was interrupted.

"Excuse me, can I talk to you for a second." The guy said.

"Sure," Jabari said.

"Come on Nephew." Yolanda said, as she got Cannon back from Jabari. "We'll be around. Hopefully, I get to see you again before we leave." She told him.

"I'm sure you will. Have fun. Oh, and make sure my mom gets to see him too before you leave."

"Yea, I'm about to take him to Cain now. I don't know where Sofia is at." She said while scoping the crowd, as she walked off.

"Hey, sorry 'bout that. Wassup?" Jabari told the guy, giving him his undivided attention.

Fallin' In Love With The Goat 3

The guy held out his hand to shake Jabari's. "Wassup, I'm Leo, Mar's cousin."

Jabari immediately frowned. "Mar's cousin?" he said. "What brings you here tonight?"

"I just came to pay my respects. I know my cousin was in love with your sister once upon a time. So, I'm here paying my respects to her and to him, since he just disappeared off the face of the earth."

"Oh," Jabari said, as he eyed Leo up and down. He didn't know what his motive was, but he didn't trust him one bit. "Why is this the first time we're meeting?"

"Because I don't live around here. I live in California where I was hoping my cousin would join me, but he never showed up. It's been 5 years and I've yet to hear from him."

"Well, I don't think this is the time or the place to discuss that." Jabari told him, as he looked around the party.

"It's not, but I spoke with Slick—"

"Slick?" Jabari pondered with an even more uneasy feeling in his gut. "You talked to Slick, when?"

"When he came out to Cali to visit with some of his people. Nevertheless, this isn't the time or the place to have this conversation, so I'm going to let you get back to your family and guests, but I really want to speak with you again, sooner than later."

"I'd like that too." Jabari told him.

"Here's my card. Call me when you have time. I'll be here for a week before going back."

By: Tiece

"A'ight," Jabari said. As Leo walked off, Karen walked up. "Hey Son, your father wants to speak with you and your brothers."

"Now? About what?"

"I don't know, but please go see what he wants. He's down the hall and in the last room on the left." She told him.

"Okay, Ma." Jabari said. The night was getting stranger and stranger. He didn't know what was going on. He looked through the crowd to see Papers and Bruno also heading down the hallway. His frazzled thoughts started traveling in all directions, not knowing what was going on or which way to go. He scanned the crowd again, looking for Leo, but he had seemed to disappear in thin air, kind of similar to his cousin. He shook his head, with an uneasy gut. *What the fuck is going on now?* He pondered to himself.

"Where the hell is your brother?" Biggs asked, as he peeked his head out of the room door.

"I don't know. I figured he'd be right behind me," Justin responded, as he sat down.

"Hell, we've been waiting for about 10 minutes." Papers said. "His slow ass. Probably out there still drinking and dancing."

"Y'all know how Cain is when he gets lit." Jabari uttered. "Bruno you good?"

"Yea," Bruno responded.

"Looks like you've had one too many yourself." Jabari teased.

"I have," Bruno admitted, as Jabari and Justin laughed.

Fallin' In Love With The Goat 3

Cain rushed into the room like he knew he was late and about to get chewed out.

"Bout time," Biggs told him. "What was the hold up?"

"Well, um." Cain stuttered. He didn't think it was appropriate for him to tell them that Lauren had hemmed him up in the bathroom and sucked his dick until he oozed down her throat. "Um, I got distracted for a moment. Sorry 'bout that Pops. So, wassup? Why we in here?" he asked, looking from one person to the other.

"Y'all know that Slick's death has been playing heavily on my mind. Not only that, but Skylar's death has also been riding me like a bad nightmare that just won't go away. I honestly feel that the two are connected, and we're gonna get to the bottom of it. It's going to take more than just me and Papers combing the streets because nobody knows nothing, at least that's all we're hearing. So, we have to take a different approach. We need all the resources we can get, even those from Skylar's cold case files."

"I agree." Papers chimed in.

"What you mean, from her cold case files?" Bruno questioned.

"I mean, I'm going to the new lead detective that is over Skylar's case to see what evidence we overlooked. I believe I now know where it lies. I just hope that the resources is there to help us figure this out."

"What resources might that be?" Jabari pondered.

"Skylar was 7 months pregnant, or close to it. I don't believe that baby was Mar's."

"What?" Justin uttered with a confused expression.

"Wow," Jabari whispered.

By: Tiece

"Come to think of it, the last conversation we had Skylar said that she had started talking to somebody new. I thought she was only joking, but maybe she was right and that somebody new could've been the baby's real father."

"Yea, but if that was the case then Mars would have probably been the culprit because he was in his feelings." Bruno said.

"But did he know?" Biggs pondered, thinking that Mars never mentioned anything about Skylar's pregnancy the entire time he was being interrogated by him and Papers. "I mean, hell, we didn't know. Maybe she didn't tell him. The public didn't even know after her death because we asked to have that information sealed."

"Interesting point." Justin said.

"What's even more interesting is that Mar's cousin Leo is here." Jabari informed them.

Papers frowned. "Is here where and why?" he asked.

"I don't know where he's at now, but he said that he needed to talk with me. I assume it's about Mars. Also, he is the one that spoke with Slick when Slick went out west to visit his family."

"What?" Cain pondered. He'd been so dazed out still thinking about the amazing head that Lauren had just gave him that he wasn't paying much attention. But hearing about Slick talking to Mar's cousin snapped him back to reality.

"Yea, he told me all that. But, we both agreed that this wasn't the time or the place."

"Well, you need to talk with him as soon as possible. I wanna know what this young man has to say about his cousin and why he showed up here to my daughter's celebration."

"Yea nephew, you need to do that asap." Papers said.

"I will," Jabari responded.

"It's something that we're overlooking and whatever that something is will lead us to all the answers we need to know." Papers told them.

"And whatever that is it has something to do with Skylar's pregnancy. I believe that will tell us if Mars was indeed the father. However, I'm starting to have a strong feeling that he wasn't. We never had her baby tested, but there should be samples somewhere that they can test, including Mar's DNA. He was questioned several times. He had to submit his DNA to clear himself, which he passed all tests that were thrown his way, so we're going to use that to see if he really was the father."

"And, if he wasn't?" Bruno asked with a curious expression on his face.

"Then the real father knows more than we think he do." Biggs answered.

"Maybe he didn't want the baby and that's why he killed her. We see this kind of shit all the time on the ID channel." Cain cut in. "Lauren be watching that shit."

Jabari shook his head, as he cut his eyes over at his brother. "The ID channel, Bruh?"

"Yea," Cain responded with serious eyes.

"Well, I guess you got a point." Jabari agreed.

"I'll keep y'all detailed and Jabari the minute you link with Mar's cousin, you let me know. Something is up with that. With him showing up here like that, it's gotta be."

By: Tiece

"A'ight Pops, I got you."

"The night is still young, so let's go celebrate Skylar's life. I have a speech to make in about 10 minutes. I don't wanna be late for that or your mom will kill me." He told them.

"Like we need another death on our hands." Cain uttered.

"Really Bruh?" Justin asked with a shake of the head.

"I'm just saying." Cain shrugged.

"Well, I have a hot date that's waiting on me. So, I'm out." Justin said, as he was first to exit the room.

"Pops your grandson and granddaughter are out there for a little while."

Biggs smiled. "Make sure I see them tonight before they leave."

"Oh, I will." Cain assured him. "Ma had Cannon by the time I was heading in here. I hope my daughter is still out there somewhere. Her mom don't be playing around. I was glad she showed up though."

"Yea, make sure I meet her too before they leave." Jabari said. "Well, I need to go check on Cash. She had her lips poked out earlier."

"I saw that," Cain cut in. "She didn't like you escorting Tiana in here."

"I know, but she'll be alright." Jabari said, as he left the room with Cain following him.

Bruno sat back sipping from his straight Hennessy with all types of thoughts running through his mind. He quietly watched as Biggs and Papers left the room. Talking about Skylar always did something to him. He had mad love for her in more ways than any of the family knew and it broke his heart to know that she'd left this earth in such a tragic way. He stared out the window and up into the sky. "Damn, Skylar I miss you." He couldn't help but reminisce about the last time they were together.

"You missed me?" Skylar asked, as she entered the trailer that she and Bruno always met in. She wasted no time walking over and giving him the biggest hug ever.

He kissed her softly on the lips. "Hell yea, I missed you. Where you been? You're like an hour late." He said, looking at his watch.

"I know. I had to talk with Mom and Pops."

"How did that go? I hope you didn't mention that we were skipping town tomorrow."

"Hell no. I did tell my brothers though. Well, Justin and Jabari."

"Why would you do that?" Bruno pondered with a frown on his face.

"I didn't tell them with who. I just said that I was leaving town." She explained.

"Damn babe. I hate you did that. I wish you would've waited."

"I'm actually glad I didn't because talking to them allowed me to come to my senses."

"What you mean by that?"

"Well," she said while walking off and fidgeting with her hands. "You're really not going to like this."

"What?" Bruno anxiously pondered.

"I told Justin and Jabari that I was pregnant."

By: Tiece

"What?!" Bruno said, as he began to pace back and forth. "You can't do that right now."

"Well, I did." Skylar told him. "I also told my parents."

Bruno shot Skylar a mean stare. "Are you fucking kidding me?!"

"Babe calm down. They were going to find out anyway."

"And, when they did we'd be far away." He told her.

"Listen at yourself. I'll be turning 19 in a few hours; you're fucking 33 years old. You should know better. I don't wanna leave my family and I don't wanna have my baby and they can't be a part of her life. You've been putting so much pressure on me to keep our relationship hidden and it's not fair anymore. I have to be honest with them about everything. Maybe not about you right now, but eventually the truth will come out."

"You don't understand. We've been fucking around since you were 16. If your father and your uncle knew that they'd have me killed."

"You're being dramatic. I'm grown now."

"Yea, but it's the principle. That can never come out."

"So, what were you thinking? We were just going to move, and I'd never come back? I mean, I know I say crazy shit when I'm mad, but I would never leave my family for good."

Bruno stood at the window looking out of it. He didn't know what to think. His brilliant idea wasn't so brilliant at all. He really didn't know what he was thinking besides not being killed by Skylar's father.

Fallin' In Love With The Goat 3

"I'm sorry." He told her, as he walked over and gave her a hug. *"I didn't mean to pressure you. I know you've been doing things for years that clearly you didn't want to do. Like leading Mars on to throw your parents off my tracks."*

"Yea, and we've been doing that so long till I don't know what's real and what's not." She told him. *"Hell, sometimes I think I even confuse him."*

"But you're not confused about this baby are you?"

"No, I know who my child's father is." She told him.

"You better." He teased. *"You're going to eventually have to tell Mars the truth, though."*

"That would include telling him everything. You ready for that, because he's gonna tell it. Especially when he learns I'm pregnant and it's not by him. Plus, have you told your wife yet?"

"I was planning on leaving with you, so what does that tell you?"

"That just tells me that you were leaving with me. It don't say nothing about you telling your wife shit."

"Don't start Skylar."

"I'm just saying. So, that's on you. If you wanna keep playing these games then I'll keep playing them too. Which means that Mars will pass as being my daughter's father."

"You must be foolish. That ain't gon' happen!"

"Well, you better figure something out and you got until tomorrow to do so."

"Are you serious?"

By: Tiece

"Hell yea, I'm serious." She told him. "I can't keep doing this. I wanna start a family of my own and I'd prefer it be with you, but if you can't bring this relationship out to the world, then I'm out of it. Me and my baby," she told him with a serious stare.

"So, you're giving me an ultimatum?"

"Yep," she said. "I am."

"You're willing to risk my life?"

"Yep, to live mine peacefully," she answered. "They don't have to know that we've been fucking around since I was 16. We could always tell them that we started seeing each other when I was 18."

"You really think that's gon' make a difference? You're still his baby girl and I'm still a married, grown ass man."

"Well, babe I don't know what to tell you. The choice is yours." She said, while looking down at her watch. "I can't keep living like this."

Bruno stood there for a minute. He loved Skylar. Unfortunately, he wasn't ready for her parents or nobody else to know. However, he knew he couldn't keep her from living the life she deserved, but he didn't feel that Mars was right for her either.

"I want you to be happy and I wish it could be with me, but nobody can ever know that we were together. I have too much to lose."

"Wow," Skyla uttered. "It's like that?"

"It has to be." Bruno told her. "I guess you're going to keep up this charade with Mars?"

Fallin' In Love With The Goat 3

"No, I'm telling Mars it's over tonight. As a matter of fact, he's supposed to meet me out here?"

"Out here?"

"Yea."

"Damn, Skylar! You doing too much! What if that nigga pulls up and I'm out here?"

"Well, you better leave then." She said, with her hand on her hip. "You better be glad I have compassion for your situation, or I would out your ass myself. You've played with my emotions long enough. You never wanted my parents to know about you and that's fucked up. I mean, I can understand you not wanting them to know back when we first started fucking around, but damn I'm grown now. If you were gonna be like this, you should've told me, and I could've been shook you out my system. I don't even believe you were ever leaving your wife! Was that all a lie too just to get me away from my people so you could control the situation?"

"I don't wanna hear this right now."

"I bet you don't. The only time we're good is when I'm doing what you want me to do. The only time we're not arguing is when we're having sex. You've played with my mental long enough and I'm over it."

"Fine time for you to say that now that you're pregnant."

"Whatever," Skylar said, and as Bruno attempted to walk out she hauled off and busted him in the back of the head with her fist. "You dirty muthafucka! You basically used me and now I'm pregnant with your baby and you wanna walk out and leave me."

By: Tiece

"You don't know who the fucking father is. Don't kid me. You were fucking Mars too."

"And, you were still fucking your wife!" she yelled, slapping him across the face.

Bruno reached back to hit her but caught himself.

"Yea hit me. I'll make sure my father knows about us."

"You threatening me?"

"Yep," Skylar said.

"Babe, are you coming to party with me or not?" Bruno's wife asked, as she entered the room, interrupting his thoughts. "Biggs told me you were in here."

Bruno cleared his throat. "Yea, I'm coming."

"You alright?"

"Yea, I'm good." He answered, but he wasn't good. He wasn't good at all. It was way too much going on for him to stay focused, but he had to get a grip and figure out his next move, because if he didn't think it out carefully, it could be his last.

Jabari sat at the bar waiting for him and Tiana's drink. He noticed Bruno and his wife heading out on the dance floor. For some reason, Bruno's whole demeanor had been off and it all started around the time Slick was killed. Although, he felt it impossible for Bruno to have something to do with Slick's death, he still couldn't help but wonder. Everybody was now suspect, including members of the crew that his father trusted. Besides blood, no one was to be trusted and Bruno was numeral Uno on his list. He needed to know what was really going on with him and the sooner the better.

"Hey, Jabari," a light voice said from behind.

"Hey Tiny." Jabari said, as he turned to face her. "How are you? I'm glad to see that you came out tonight."

"Yea, I wouldn't have missed it for the world." She said.

"You want me to order you a drink?"

Tiny held up her glass. "Nah, this is like my second one already. I need to pace myself." She grinned.

"I feel you. So, what's up? The last time we saw each other you acted like you had something you wanted to get off your chest."

"Yea, I kind of did and I guess right now wouldn't be the best of timing to tell you. I did stop by your parents' house, but you weren't there. I left my number with your mom to call me, but you never did." She said.

"I'm sure she forgot to tell me. She be having so much on her mind. Sorry 'bout that. But, you good? What'd you need to talk with me about?" *Oh God,* Jabari thought just as he spotted Cashmere eyeing him down from across the room.

"Well, what I wanted to say I really couldn't at the doctor's office. Not while your girl was there," she said.

"Who? Cashmere?" he frowned.

"Yea."

"And, why is that?" he asked, just as he could see Cashmere heading his way.

"Because that baby might not be yours."

By: Tiece

Jabari frowned with an uncertain expression on his face. "Say what now?" he asked.

"I said—"

"Heyyy, so we meet again," Cashmere butted in, as she walked up invading their conversation.

"Heyyy," Tiny nervously smiled. She looked at Jabari with an uneasy expression on her face.

"I'm not interrupting anything important am I?" Cashmere asked.

"No," Tiny quickly answered, and then looked over at Jabari. "We'll catch up later. I ain't going nowhere."

Jabari nodded his head as an indication that it was cool for her to walk off, but he stared at Cashmere with bothered eyes.

"You good? You a'ight?" Cashmere asked, trying not to show how concerned she really was.

"Yea," Jabari told her. He had no plans to make the night any worse by bringing up what Tiny had just said. However, he couldn't take his mind off it. What could Tiny be talking about and how would she possibly know anything about Cashmere besides her once being his lady? He shook his head with uneasy thoughts, as the bartender bought over his drinks.

"Well, I know that ain't for me." Cashmere joked.

"Nah, it's not. But hey, I hope you're enjoying yourself. I'll catch up with you later." He told her and just like that, he walked off. Now wasn't the time for him to go into details that even he was unsure about, but one thing was for sure. Every dog had its day, and Cashmere's was coming. What she didn't know was that it would be sooner than later if she was lying to him about the baby she was carrying. Only time or the truth would tell, and he was hell bent on getting to the bottom of everything that could compromise his happiness or his freedom.

By: Tiece

Chapter One

It was early morning, as Jabari drove around with all kinds of thoughts playing on his mental. He took in a deep breath and then let it out, as he tried his best to hide the anger he felt inside. It had been a week after the party, and much too long for him to have something so serious weighing on his heart. Ironically, he didn't even try to get in touch with Tiny simply because if it was something that serious to tell he'd rather give Cashmere a chance to come clean. More importantly, how would Tiny know that Cashmere's baby might not be his? It was the million-dollar question that just wouldn't let his mind rest. Did she see Cashmere somewhere and if she had where at? Who was she with? How long had she known about this? Question after question, and still no solid answers, but he planned on getting some sooner than later.

As he sat there thinking, his cell phone began to ring. He looked down at the caller ID to see that it was Cain. Without hesitation, he answered.

"Wassup Bruh?"

"Wassup B. What you doing?"

"Just rolling right now, you good?"

"Hell yea, I just been chilling and enjoying this spontaneous mood Lauren been in."

Jabari grinned. "Damn, she still fucking yo' brains out?"

Fallin' In Love With The Goat 3

"Bruuuuuh, I don't know what's gotten into her, but I love it. You know that saying, a man loves sex until he meets a woman that loves it more?"

"Yea."

"Well, I know they lyin'! It's the best thing she could've ever done."

Jabari grinned.

"This morning I'm in the shower right, eyes closed, water running down my back and the next thing I know, she's behind me. I didn't even hear her get in, all I felt was her body against mine when she wrapped her arms around me. Shit, you know from there it was on."

"Nigga, you don't get tired?"

"Hell no. Have you seen my lady? Shit, Lauren still turns me on. She don't get older she gets younger with age. You ever met a woman like that? Oh, my bad. The relationship you had with Cashmere was the longest one you ever held down and she's still in her mid 20's. So, you probably haven't." He joked.

"That sounds about right." Jabari agreed. "But, don't get me wrong, Cash is sexy as fuck too. Yea, she's younger than Lauren, but I can see age being good to her. More importantly, Tiana and Lauren are sisters and honestly she looks like she's in her early twenties. That shit must run in their family. My wood gets hard every time I'm around Tiana. I can't help myself."

Cain laughed. "I know the feeling B. Just to think, Lauren wasn't as open and free about sex. Suddenly, she's like a crazed woman in and out the bedroom, but in a good way."

By: Tiece

"Honestly, I think Lauren is pleasing you more to make sure no one else is doing her job."

"I've definitely thought about it and you're probably right." Cain agreed.

"Well, what I'm trying to tell you is that you need to have a talk with her to let her know that no one is taking her place. You need to make it clear that you don't want your kids' mothers', but that it's all about her and your kids. Nothing more or less."

"I hear you, B."

"I just don't want you to get used to her acting like this when it could be just a phase. Lauren is still going through something. She's still hurt behind you having 2 kids on her, when y'all ain't even had 1 yet."

"You right."

"So, be careful with that."

"I will," Cain told him. "I completely understand where you're coming from and I'll have a talk with her about that."

"Cool," Jabari said. "But aye, what you know about Yolanda?"

"Who?"

"Yolanda, Sophia's sister? Yo' baby mama."

"Oh, YoYo? She's a cool chick. Hell, she practically keeps my son. Every time I turn around he's with her."

"Yea, I peeped that just from the little conversation we've had. What she do for a living? She got a man?"

Fallin' In Love With The Goat 3

"Nah, I don't believe she's in a relationship. Not that I know of," he added. "But she works from home building websites and shit like that. From what Sofia tells me, she makes really good money."

"Damn, must be nice. Reminds me of Tiana with that working from home."

"Yea, both of 'em work from home. You will find you some independent women that be doing the damn thang."

"I guess," Jabari uttered.

"So, you like YoYo too?"

Jabari grinned. "YoYo, that's funny."

"Hell, that's what I always hear Sofia call her."

"Anyway, I do like her but I'm chilling right now. I wouldn't mind getting to know her. You know, I like me some Tiana, I ain't gon' lie, but I ain't settled down with nobody. I'm entitled to live and enjoy myself."

"You got that right. I would suggest that's what you do, too. Just protect yourself and don't be making babies with this woman and that woman. Don't be a fool like yo' brother." Cain preached.

"Nah, I'm definitely not gonna do that. Cash getting pregnant was a surprise to me because she's been on the pill for a long time. Speaking of Cash, I'm heading to her house now. We need to talk."

"You ain't about to ask her about that shit Tiny was talking about are you?"

"Hell yea, I'm tired of this shit weighing on my mind."

"You sho' you wanna do that? I mean, damn what the hell could Tiny know anyway? Unless she saw her out with somebody. Plus, the woman is pregnant. Hell, you're gonna get a DNA test anyway—"

"I know, but I don't wanna get too attached to this baby before it gets here and then it's not mine."

"Think about it B. Whether you had talked to Tiny or not, you were still chilling with her and you even went to a doctor's appointment. Regardless, you're getting close to that baby. So, I really don't think that what Tiny said should matter much. You already had your suspicions before Tiny showed up. You're already getting tested, so that's why I say it shouldn't matter."

"It matters to me."

"Yea, well, I feel you. However, I don't think it should. I ain't gon' lie. I kinda feel sorry for shawty. She's been catching hell as is from you."

"I don't agree."

"I'm sure you don't but think about it. You already dipped on her before the baby even came into the picture. You didn't have any solid proof that she was cheating on you, yet you hauled ass anyway. If it's not true, I'm sure she's had a hard time dealing with that—"

"Yea, but it's true. I might not be able to pinpoint it, but it's fucking true." Jabari told him.

"Okaaay,"

Jabari glanced down at his phone to see that Tiny was calling him. "Damn, this couldn't be better timing."

"Why you say that?"

"Tiny is beeping in."

"Nooooo," Cain said.

"It's her because I locked her number in when I stopped by to see mom's. However, I did tell Ma if she stops back by just give her my number and tell her to call me. Honestly, I didn't want to reach out to her, because I'd rather get some straight-forward answers from Cash. However, I also felt like if Tiny showed back up then what she was saying needed to be heard."

"So, you gon' answer that and see what she's talking about?"

"Nah, I'm gon' wait until I go in here and holla at Cash first." He said, pulling up in Cashmere's driveway. "I need to give her the opportunity to tell me the truth and if she don't, then I'll call Tiny and put her on speaker right there in her face."

"Damn B, you gon' do it like that?"

"Yep, I have no choice. One thing Cash ain't gon' do is keep making a fool out of me. I need to know the truth. Shit might hurt a lil bit, but I'm prepared for it."

"Wow, this shit is crazy. I think you should give her a break."

"I was giving her a break until Tiny hit me with the shit at the party. I wasn't expecting that."

"Tiny should've kept her big mouth closed. That party wasn't the time or the place for that. I still can't even imagine how the hell she could come to the conclusion that Cashmere's baby ain't yours."

"I don't know either, but I need to get to the bottom of it."

"A'ight Bruh." Cain irritably uttered. "If shawty go into early labor blame yourself because you're putting a lot of pressure on her."

By: Tiece

"Ain't no pressure if Cash ain't fucked nobody else. She'll stick to her truth and when that baby is born it'll be mine."

"A'ight, since you won't listen to me I hope this works out for you. I just don't see nobody winning here. I really don't."

"I hear you Bruh. But look, I'll hit you back when I leave here."

"Make sure you do." Cain said, and with that Jabari ended their call.

Jabari wasted no time getting out of the car and making his way up the stairs to Cashmere's front door. The minute he reached the door, she opened it.

"Damn, you must've saw me pulling up." He said.

Cashmere smiled. "Yea, I had just opened the blinds in here. Why you ain't call first? I could've had a nigga over." She teased.

"Well, maybe now ain't the time to be playing about something like that." He told her with a serious expression.

Cashmere rolled her eyes with an irritated shake of the head. "Can't even joke with you now?" she pondered. "Okay, what brings you by?"

Jabari hadn't quite found the words yet.

"So, wassup B? You've been acting funny since your sister's party. I assume you wanna talk to me about something."

Jabari nodded his head. "Yea, I guess you can say that."

"Well, funny thing is that I wanna talk with you about something too." She told him. "Have a seat."

Fallin' In Love With The Goat 3

Jabari was somewhat shocked. He didn't know what Cashmere wanted to talk with him about, but he was all ears as he sat down to listen. "Wassup?"

"Well, let me grab you something to drink first." She said, heading into the kitchen.

"Nah, I'm good," he said stopping her. "Let's talk."

"Okay," Cashmere said. "It's some things I feel the need to get off my chest. I'm tired of walking on eggshells around you or trying to be Miss Perfect so you don't be tripping or acting weird. More importantly, it's not good for the baby and I never thought I'd feel this way, but my baby, this baby," she emphasized rubbing her stomach, "is the most important person to me in the world. Anything I do from this point on is and will always be in the best interest of my baby."

Jabari sat there watching her. Was she going to come clean about the very thing he'd been pressing her so hard about? He didn't know what was about to come to light, but he was sitting on the edge of his seat waiting to hear it.

"One thing about secrets I've learned is that they lose their power once they're exposed and well, I'm done with mine. I'm tired of the lies." Cashmere said, while sitting across from Jabari. She didn't want to sit too close.

"Wow," Jabari mumbled under his breath. He'd been waiting for Cashmere to come clean, but in all honesty he wasn't ready for it if she was.

"Well, um" Cashmere uttered, just as Jabari's cell phone began to ring again. He glanced down at the display screen to see that it was Tiny calling back. At that moment, he really wanted to answer it but Cashmere intervened.

"I see that's Tiny calling you," she said, as she could see the name on his display screen.

"Yea, it's her. Is there something that Tiny knows that I don't know? Is that the thing on your chest that you can't wait to get off?" Jabari pondered, figuring that Cashmere was no fool.

She nodded her head, and then answered. "Maybe," she said, in a soft, subtle, nervous tone.

Jabri frowned. "Okay and what you mean by that?"

Cashmere sat twiddling her fingers, while fearfully shaking her legs.

"Well," Jabari said, giving her the side-eye.

"Well," she hesitated in thinking what it was she really wanted to say. As she stared in Jabari's eyes she knew once she revealed her secrets that he'd never look at her the same. She rubbed her hand softly across her stomach, knowing that this was something she had to do for her baby. It was now or never. "Well, um."

"Damn, just say it, Cash!"

"When you were locked up I leaned on someone that was here for me. He listened to me, gave me sound advice and he helped me get through some tough times. Even during our break-up, not long ago he was there for me."

"He?" Jabari pondered. "He huh?"

Fallin' In Love With The Goat 3

"Yes, and um. He was just a really good friend to me. I, well, we never expected things to go any further than that, but one night it did."

Jabari's facial expression turned cold, as anger began to seep in.

"Please, just hear me out." Cashmere pleaded.

By: Tiece

Chapter Two

Cashmere sat on the edge of the chair not wanting Jabari to cut in and stop her or she wouldn't be able to finish her truth, well not exactly the whole truth. "It was after our break-up and I was taking things really hard. I struggled with you leaving me and I didn't know how to deal with it. So, I called him, and we met up to talk. He and I were drinking and talking. I was crying and upset, he was trying to comfort me, and then one thing led to another and before I knew it things had gone too far." She half-heartedly admitted.

"Things went too far? So, you're saying you cheated on me?"

"Technically, we weren't together." She slid in. "However, I'm sure you'll still see it the way you want to see it."

"You got that right." Jabari responded in an annoyed tone. "So, we broke up and you fucked somebody else?"

Cashmere shrugged her shoulders. "It didn't quite happen like that, but unfortunately—"

"You fucked somebody else." He cut in to finish her sentence, but in a harsher tone. "So, you don't know who's the father of your baby?"

Cashmere's eyes filled with water. "I know it's you."

"No, the fuck you don't!" Jabari said, with a raised unpleasant tone. "No, you don't!"

"Yes, I do." She began to cry.

Jabari shook his head. "How do you know Cash? What's the timeline? How can you be sure this baby isn't somebody's else's?"

"I can feel it, Jabari. I just know it."

"But you're not 100% sure are you?" Jabari questioned, as he stood up. "Just keep it muthafuckin' real with me. Could this baby be another nigga's?" he questioned, just as his phone chirped of an incoming text message. He didn't even bother to look down at it because he was too busy staring in Cashmere's face, waiting for the whole truth and nothing but the truth. "Are you sure?" he asked again.

"In my heart I'm sure."

"But in reality you're not? Just say it Cash! I'm already pissed off! Do you wanna make this shit worse than what it already is?"

"No," Cashmere answered, as she continued to cry. She had come that far and it was much too late to turn back now. The only thing she could do was come clean in hopes that one day he'd forgive her.

"Could this be another nigga's baby?"

"Yes," Cashmere responded. "Yes, it could be." She answered, just as Jabari's phone began to ring again. This time he glanced down at the display of his phone screen to see that it was Tiny calling again. He shook his head with saddened, frustrated thoughts.

"And what does this *HE* have to do with Tiny?" Jabari asked, almost already getting sick to his stomach.

"*HE* is Tiny's cousin."

By: Tiece

Jabari instantly felt sick, as if he wanted to throw up. All kinds of memories began to plague his thoughts, mostly bad and in what he'd heard. Things that he turned a blind eye to just because he didn't want to believe it. Had his best friend been playing him all along? Was the shit going on the whole time he was locked up? She said it only happened once, but a part of him was saying it had happened many times. His eyes filled with tears; angry, disappointed tears. "So, you mean to tell me that—" he paused, almost getting choked up. It was too hard to even say it. He'd felt played and betrayed by the one person in the world that was the closest to him. The one person that knew exactly how he felt about Cashmere.

"Yes, the person I had a moment with was Slick." Cashmere confessed, even though she didn't want to.

"A moment? Is that what you're calling it now? A fucking moment?!" He asked, walking up on her.

"Jabari calm down. Please, you're scaring me," she begged, as Jabari swung over by the end table and knocked the lamp on the floor. The vase of the lamp shattered into pieces causing Cashmere to scream out in fear.

"So, you and Slick was fucking behind my back?!"

"It wasn't like that!"

"Yes, the fuck it was! You mean to tell me that you and my best friend was fucking this entire time?!"

"NO, it wasn't like that." Cashmere cried. She was scared to death because the look in Jabari's eyes was one that she'd never seen before. It was a look that said if he could kill her he would with no regrets about it.

"Wow, you actually fucked my best friend, my brother?" Jabari uttered. He sadly shook his head, as a tear fell from his eye. More than anything, he was heartbroken that she and Slick had taken it there. It was almost unbelievable, but he was for sure that she wasn't lying. She wouldn't risk her life or the baby's life to confess something so serious in nature that it could get her knocked off. "How many times?"

"Once," she answered.

"You lying."

"No, I'm not." She cried.

"You are lying!" he yelled out, while punching a hole in her living room wall.

Cashmere screamed out again, this time scurrying down the long, narrow hallway and into her bedroom. Quickly, she locked the door. "Jabari, please leave. I don't wanna have to call the police on you." She cried from behind the bedroom door. "Please, leave!" she yelled out through nervous tears.

It had gotten quiet, as she stood there silently praying that her life wasn't in danger. A minute felt like an hour, and then the sound of his car could be heard as the engine started. She dashed over to the window to peek out of it, catching the tail end of Jabari's car hauling ass out of her neighborhood. She took in a deep breath and then let it back out. She had done something she never in a million years thought she'd do. It almost cost her everything, but she felt it was more than necessary. Plus, if she didn't tell it Tiny would have, and she'd rather it came from her then a nosey bitch on the outside. She tensely grabbed her stomach, somewhat relieved that the truth was out about the baby, but still deeply in her feelings. She shook her head, while sitting on the side of her bed.

"Why did you have to tell Tiny about us Slick?! I told you that this shit would come back to bite us in the ass. But nah, you had to tell somebody. Lucky for you, your ass ain't here to deal with it!" she spat like Slick was in the room with her, as thoughts of Jabari crossed her mind. "Damn, I pray someday he'll forgive me. Please Lord, let this baby be his."

After she got herself together a couple of hours later, Cashmere found herself pulling up to Shyla's house. She swerved in behind a few parked cars that were lined up on the side of the road. As always, anytime she had problems, Shyla always had a way of distracting her load even if it was just for the moment. She grabbed her purse and then stepped out of the car. "Hello." She spoke to a lady that had passed her, while walking up in Shyla's driveway.

Cashmere scoped out the scenery, as she spotted Net. "Hey Auntie." She said, throwing her hand in the air while waving.

"Hey Cash." Net called out, as she looked up but then continued to assist a neighbor that was looking at a desk and a swivel chair.

"Hey Bestie," Shyla called out, calling Cashmere over.

Cashmere smiled with a shake of the head, as she made her way over to Shyla. "What the fuck?" she questioned, while looking at all the people in the yard shopping. "I know you said you was having a yard sale, but damn bitch is this your whole fucking house?" she joked.

Shyla grinned. "Not exactly." She answered, while looking over at a neighbor that was holding up a golf set. "That's one-hundred-dollars," she told the guy. "I'll throw in the golf attire too for another fifty. You look like you can fit those outfits. They'll look good on you." She said with a winning smile.

"Wow, you wasn't bullshitting Bestie." Cashmere uttered. "OMG, are you seriously getting rid of that living room furniture?" she asked, just as she spotted it over by the garage. "That shit is bad ass. Hell, I would've bought it if I'd known you were going to do this with it."

"Bitch, I just gave you a bad ass living room suit. Chill out, let somebody else get it. Hell, they paying way more than what yo' ass would've been trying to give me for it anyway."

"Who said I was paying?"

"See, that's what I'm saying." Shyla grinned.

"I can't believe you're getting rid of it though."

"I don't want shit out of Rich's house; especially one he shared with his wife. For all I know he has brought a lot of shit over here from over there. Plus, I have a neighbor that's coming back to get it. You see the sold sign on it, right? He's paying me three-thousand-dollars for it."

"Daaaaamn, that's good."

"Hell, it originally cost seven-thousand and my neighbor knew it. So, he was well aware that he was getting a deal, deal."

"I see," Cashmere nodded with an approving smile. "Rich ass gon' be mad as hell when he visits and notices all of his shit is gone."

By: Tiece

"Who gives a fuck about Rich and or his opinions? I know I don't."

"Well, the whole neighborhood can see that." Cashmere joked. "I mean damn, you're selling the man's clothes, his shoes, the office furniture that was in his office space—"

"Yep, all that and some more. But definitely everything that's his."

"Well, luckily the kids are part yours or they'd be out here on the lawn with the rest of his shit."

Shyla laughed out loud. "You know what to say." She teased. "Maaa," she called out, as Net looked her way. "Take over for me. I'll be back." She headed inside the house, with Cashmere right behind her. The minute they stepped foot in the house, Shyla turned to face her.

"So, what the fuck happened over at your place? Bitch you've been holding out on me." She told her.

"I know, but it's not like that."

"Well, how the hell is it, because from my knowledge you claimed you hadn't been with nobody, but then you call to tell me that you confessed to Jabari that the baby may not be his? I need you to start from the top and don't leave nothing out." Shyla told her.

"Well, can we at least go somewhere and sit down." Cashmere said, as they walked through the house. "Or, is everything you sit on outside?" she joked, but was very serious being that Shyla's house looked somewhat empty.

"We going in my bedroom." Shyla told her. Once they made it in the bedroom, Shyla turned to face her. "Sit down bitch and spill the tea."

"Well," Cashmere started with an annoyed shake of the head, as she walked over and sat in the lounge chair in the corner. "I had to not only keep it real with Jabari, but I also had to keep it real with myself. The last thing I wanted to happen was for me to have the baby and it not be his."

"But bitch you assured me that it was his."

"I lied, well kind of."

Shyla shook her head with the Kanye emoji look. "Okay, carry on." She said.

"I needed to jump in front of the shit that Tiny was about to start. I couldn't have her tell some shit and make it look worse than what it really was."

"Tiny is Slick's cousin, right?"

"Yea, and I don't exactly know what she was going to tell Jabari, but I do know that it had something to do with me and Slick."

"How you figure that though? Did she see y'all together or something?"

"Well, he told her about us."

Shyla frowned. "Why would he do a dumb thing like that?" she pondered.

"Being foolish." Cashmere responded with a shake of the head. "He told me that one night him and Tiny had gotten drunk. He started feeling all mushy and shit and just blurted out how he felt about me. At first, she didn't believe him, until he made her promise to not say nothing about it and that's when she knew it was real."

"Well, the bitch sholl don't know how to hold on to her promises." Shyla uttered. "Never tell that bitch nothing."

"Right."

"So, hold up Bitch. Are you saying that this may not be Jabari's baby?"

"Well—"

"Think carefully before you answer that; especially being that you're just telling me this. Who else is in the picture Cash? Is it just Jabari and Slick OR is someone else also involved in this fiasco?"

Cashmere sat quietly pondering over her thoughts. There was only one thing that she wholeheartedly believed in and because of that she had to stick to her guns.

However, her cousin did deserve the truth. Well, at least the version in which she would confess.

Chapter Three

"Shy, I know this shouldn't be just coming out; especially with you asking me over and over again, but I didn't want to say nothing because even still I feel it's irrelevant when it comes to my baby."

"Bitch, is the baby Slick's or not?" Shyla cut in.

Cashmere shrugged. "No, it's not. Well, I don't know," she responded with confusion.

"Damn bitch! You could've told me that."

"I know I could've, but I didn't want to. You're always so hard on me and the night it happened it wasn't supposed to. Shit just kinda happened. I mean damn, we were both lit and talking foolish. Next thing I know, me and him were making out. I didn't mean for it to happen, but it did. Nevertheless, the day before, me and Jabari had just had sex—"

"Damn, you're a big-time slut." Shyla teased.

"Don't I know it." Cashmere agreed. "My hoish days are over though."

Shyla shot Cashmere the side-eye. "Once a slut, always a slut." She joked.

Cashmere laughed. "Bitch I get tired of you."

"Anyway, this is craaaaaazy as hell, Bestie. What you gonna do? I mean, what if this baby is Slick's, then what?"

By: Tiece

Cashmere sat in silence while pondering over the question. She'd thought about it but hadn't really thought about it. "Shit, I'm so confused right now."

"Better yet, let's back up Bitch. What the fuck did Jabari say?!" Shyla asked, as if that should've been first on her list of questions, but the news about Slick possibly being the father had taken precedence.

"He was hurt. I mean, really hurt. He took it out on my lamp."

Shyla frowned. "Whet?!" she asked with sarcasm. "What you mean by that?"

"He swung on my lamp and broke it into pieces. Literally, scared the shit out of me."

"You shitted yourself?"

"No Bitch! But he scared the shit out of me, not fucking literally but still." Cashmere responded with a roll of the eyes. "Didn't I say I'm 'bout tired of yo' ass."

Shyla grinned. "I'm just kidding Bestie. Trying to lighten your load."

"Ha, ha, is that better?"

"Nah, but moving on. Did Jabari leave after he killed yo' lamp?"

"Hell nawl, he punched a fucking hole in my living room wall too. I didn't even stick around after that. I hauled ass into the bedroom and told him to leave or I was calling the police."

"The police? Damn, you was scared."

"Hell yea, I never saw him act like that before. He's usually so cool, calm and collective, but all that shit was thrown out the window when I decided to be honest for a change."

Shyla frowned. "So, you told him that you'd been fucking Slick, all up in y'all's bed and while he was locked up?"

"No, I didn't tell him all that. Some shit I refused to tell him. All I know is that I needed to get in front of Tiny and her news. I'd rather he hear it from me than her."

"Well, I must give you props on that. You're a better woman than me because I would've kept that shit under wraps as long as I could've."

"Yea, but Tiny was making sure that it wouldn't go under wraps for long. She even called him while he was at my house."

Shyla's eyes stretched. "Before or after he showed his ass?"

"Right before I gave him the tea." Cashmere responded. "Hell, I could feel she was about to out me. Luckily, he didn't answer. That gave me enough time to tell him."

"Damn, the bitch that pressed to wanna fuck up your shit? Her cousin is dead and gone, he couldn't take care of a baby if he wanted to. So, why she wanna be so messy? I mean, that's really fucked up and speaks volumes as to what kind of shade tree bitch she really is."

"Exactly."

"If we're ever out somewhere and you see her, just point her out. I'm gon' whoop her muthafuckin' ass just on the strength that she tried you like that."

By: Tiece

Cashmere grinned. "Oh, just because I'm pregnant doesn't mean that I'm not going to get in a kick or two."

"Shit, you know how we roll." Shyla laughed. "But damn, I feel bad for my boy. You ain't talk to him no more?"

"Not since he left earlier this morning. I don't know where he's at or what he's doing. He might be somewhere talking shit about me. Got me looking like a real slut out in these streets."

"Well, bitch if the shoe fits, tie that muthafucka up and wear it."

Cashmere shook her head. "I'm going home with yo' salty ass. I'm sick of you."

"No, you ain't." Shyla grinned.

"But seriously, my heart is broken. I never meant for any of this to come out. I feel bad because I've hurt the man I love, and I can't take it back. He knows I've been unfaithful and with his best friend. Not only that, but I'm pregnant. This shit is bothering me Shy. I'm sick. I feel bad as hell. I'm trying not to show it because I don't wanna stress myself more than what I'm already doing, but it's hard. I'm trying to protect my baby already, but it's so fucking hard. I fucked up. I know I did, and I don't know if Jabari will ever forgive me. Even if this baby is his, he'll never look at me the same and that sickens me." Cashmere said, as tears began to fall from her eyes.

"Don't cry, Cash. You're a strong woman. You've been through hell and back and you survived. This too shall pass. You showed courage by being honest. I know that's the last thing you wanted to do but you pulled yourself together and came clean. That's gotta count for something, right?"

Cashmere shrugged her shoulders. "I guess." She said.

Fallin' In Love With The Goat 3

"You gotta pull yourself together. You have a baby inside of you. I know it's easier said than done, but you can't keep putting yourself through this. Regardless of if this baby is Jabari's or not, we gon' step. You know I'm gon' step and I know you gon' do the same. So, don't beat yourself up about this. The truth had to come out and it did. Now, you ain't gotta worry about having the baby and then finding out the hard way that it's not Jabari's. At least it won't be a shocker to him."

"But I know this baby is his." Cashmere said.

"You think it's his?"

"I know it's his. I just know it."

"You keep saying that, but I hope you're not too disappointed if you find out that it's not."

"What the hell is going on in yo' yard?!" Rich barked while barging in Shyla's room.

Cashmere's eyes stretched, as she screamed out at the sight of Rich lunging for Shyla. *What the fuck!* She thought.

"Nigga, I wish you might put yo' muthafuckin' dick beaters on me!" Shyla said, as she stopped Rich in his tracks. "What do you want?! Didn't I tell you to fucking ring the doorbell before entering my house?"

"Don't start that shit with me Shy. Why the hell are you selling shit that I bought for you?"

Shyla stood up from the bed, as Cashmere sat with her mouth partly open. She didn't know what had just happened, but whatever it was it happened fast.

By: Tiece

"First off nigga, you ain't bought me shit. For all I know, you been giving me shit that you bought your wife. She wanted a new bedroom suit, maybe you gave me y'all old one for my guest room here."

"You sound crazy." Rich cut in, and then noticed Cashmere sitting in the lounge chair over in the corner. "You just sitting here letting her do this foolish shit?"

Cashmere shrugged with a clueless expression. The last thing she wanted was to butt her nose in their business. She only did that with Shyla, not with Shyla and Rich. "I ain't got nothing to do with this."

"She ain't got shit to do with this!" Shyla reiterated.

"I think we need to talk." Rich said.

"I was talking to the person I wanted to talk with, and that didn't include you." Shyla told him.

Cashmere stood up. "I think I should leave."

"You ain't gotta leave. His ass is leaving." Shyla said.

"No, I'm not leaving. We need to talk." Rich said.

"Yea, I'm leaving." Cashmere said. "I have enough shit to deal with as is."

Shyla shook her head. "I'm sorry Bestie. Had I known he was coming here I would've sold this shit at your house instead of mine."

"I know you lying!" Cashmere cut in with a shake of the head, as Shyla walked her out.

"This that bullshit." Shyla uttered, once they'd made it outside. Most of the stuff in the yard was either gone or being sold. It actually went a lot faster than she thought.

"Damn, it was way more stuff out here than when I first got here. You made a really good come up I'm sure."

"I sure did, and I don't care how Rich feels about it."

"Girl, you got your hands full. Do you need me to stay for back-up? I'll crack the nigga side the head with a bottle, a frying pan, a hammer—"

Shyla laughed. "You know Rich ain't 'bout that life. I wish that nigga would put his hands on me. His ass will get fucked up and taken to jail. I don't play that shit."

Cashmere laughed out loud. She knew Shyla could very well take care of herself.

"Well, I'm gonna get on outta here. Call me later."

"I will," Shyla said. "I'm coming over. I don't think you should stay by yourself tonight."

"Awww, Bestie you're coming to stay with me?"

Shyla nodded her head. "I'll do anything for you, you know that. And, yes we'll have a sleepover tonight. I'm sure you'd love that."

"Hell yea, we can watch POWER and eat popcorn."

"You know what to say," Shyla agreed, just as Net walked over.

"What the hell is his yellow ass doing here? I thought you said it was over."

By: Tiece

"Oh Lawd, that's my queue." Cashmere intervened, as she hugged her aunt and then Shyla. "I'm outta here. I'll see you later, Shy."

"For sure." Shyla responded, as she then addressed her mother. "I don't know why he's here Ma, but come in the house with me just in case you need to crack this nigga side the head."

"I've been waiting to do that since the first day I met him."

Cashmere laughed out loud, as she looked back at Shyla and shook her head. She then wasted no time making it to her car. The last thing she needed was to be caught up in some more shit. She really didn't need that type of drama in her life. She had enough already to last her a lifetime."

Later that evening, Jabari lay in bed with all kinds of thoughts running through his head. Upset was an underestimate, as he sighed not knowing what to do at this point. After leaving Cashmere's house he rode around for a while until he ended up at the burial site where Slick's body was laid to rest. He sat out there for an hour or better trying to come up with answers, all the while not knowing that his best friend had been playing him this whole time. The only question he could ask was, how could you? His heart was definitely broken more by Slick than Cashmere. Living by the guy code was supposed to have been stronger than any relationship they'd had with a female, no matter who she was. He still couldn't believe that it had come to down to that. Now, Cashmere was pregnant and didn't know who the father was. If it would've been by anybody else he could accept that better, but because Slick was now in the picture, that pill was much harder to swallow. After feeling like he'd never get the answers he wanted, he left. Not wanting to deal with nothing or nobody, he headed back to his own crib to mull things over and if nothing else hope to sleep things off in hopes to wake up to it all being a dream.

As he lay in bed, tossing and turning his phone sounded off again. It had been going off over and over as the hours went by, but he didn't check it, nor did he want to see who it was. He simply let it ring while also ignoring the text messages. Finally, he snatched it up from the nightstand to see who all had been trying to reach out. He saw a missed call from Tiana, Papers and Justin. He shook his head noticing the three missed calls from Tiny. She just wasn't letting up.

"Damn, you can give it a rest. I know the truth now." He uttered.

He then opened his text messages.

Aye nephew, just checking on you. Hit me back when you get a chance. PAPERS

Quickly, he messaged Papers back.

Wassup Unc. Been chilling most of the day. Took a break from everybody and everything, but I'm good. I'll call you later. JAH

He moved on to the next message.

Hey Jabari. This is Tiny. Call me back when you get this message.

Jabari shook his head; he really wasn't in the mood for Tiny's shit. It was bad enough that he'd found out about Cashmere, but at least he heard it from her. It was even more embarrassing to hear it from somebody else, yet Tiny was determined to spill the beans. Even though she may have felt she was doing the right thing, she wasn't. Or, at least he just wasn't ready to hear about it again. He sighed and then moved on to the next message.

Hey Babe. Was thinking about you. Anyway, I'm hoping that we can link later. Just let me know if you have the time. TIANA

He thought about messaging her back, not really feeling up to the company, but didn't want to just leave her hanging.

Hey Beautiful. I really don't have plans. Been kinda taking some time to myself. If I decide to come out I'll let you know. JAH

Moving on to the next message.

Bruh, wyd? We're headed to Club 2. You should join me and the crew. JUSTIN

Without hesitation, he messaged back.

Wassup Bruh. I see you messaged over an hour ago. If y'all still there, I might just come out. I'll let you know in about 30 minutes. JAH

As he lay there contemplating if he should go out or not, his text message alert went off again. It was Tiny.

"What the fuck?" he said. "Shawty messy as hell." He opened the message to read it.

Hey Jabari, I've been trying to get in touch with you. I thought we would've talked by now, but I can't seem to catch you. There is no easy way to say this, but your girl was sleeping with my cousin Slick. I know for a fact that it'd been going on for quite some time, up until a few weeks before he died. I know because he told me. I didn't believe it at first, but eventually I did. Slick actually really liked her, but he didn't want to sabotage y'all's brotherhood. He loved you too much. However, he got caught up with the wrong girl.

Fallin' In Love With The Goat 3

Unfortunately, it was your girl. I couldn't sit back and watch this unfold not knowing if her baby was my cousin's; especially since he's gone. Losing him was a big blow to our whole family. I know that may sound strange being that he was always with your family, but Slick had gotten really close with all of us in the past few years and we loved him. He made sure we were straight and we appreciated it. Not only that, but you do know that he and I was always the closest two since yay high. So, if there is a chance that this baby is his I'd like to know.

I don't want to give you too much, but I don't want you to be surprised either. I'm meaning just in case the baby isn't yours or Slick's. He did mention once that he had found out she was fucking her neighbor. Some dude name Dirty. So, no telling who the baby's daddy is. I'm just praying for the best outcome. Whatever that may be. I'm praying for you too Jabari. I know losing him still weighs on you and hearing this will likely make that load heavier. I'm just sorry to be the bearer of bad news. I just felt that you needed to know. TINY

Jabari's eyes filled with hatred, while shaking his head. He wasted no time sending his supposedly, untrustworthy baby mama a text message.

Oh, so you were fucking Dirty too? JAH

By: Tiece

Chapter Four

The club was packed, as Justin made his way through the crowd and over to the VIP table where Cain, Lauren, and Sonya were seated at.

"Wassup y'all?" Justin spoke while sitting down next to Cain. Lauren and Cain nearly spoke in unison, as Cain and Justin gave each other dap.

"Hey Justin," Sonya said separately with a big smile spread across her face. "You looking good, as always."

Justin smiled back with a nod of the head. "Wassup Sonya? You look good too."

Lauren shook her head, as she tossed back her drink. "She's feeling good tonight Bruh, you better be careful."

Justin grinned. "Oh yea?"

"Yea," Sonya answered for Lauren. "You know I've missed you."

"Oh yea?" Justin coolly said again with a bashful smile and a shake of the head. His facial expression showed a chill man, but inside he wasn't feeling nothing that came out of Sonya's mouth.

Lauren could tell that Justin was a little caught off guard, not only because she was there with Cain, but because she'd brought her bestie Sonya with her. Quickly, she cut in to ease the tension. "Hey girl, let's go over to the bar and order some chicken wings. Give the guys some space to enjoy this ass." She grinned while smacking one of the dancers on the butt.

Sonya smiled, as she agreed. "Yea, girl, come on."

"You want something babe?" Lauren asked Cain.

"Nah, I'm good on the drinks and food, but stop by the ATM over in the corner behind the bar and grab me about one-hundred ones before you come back."

"Okay, will do." Lauren said, as she grabbed Sonya by the hand, leaving the men to themselves.

The minute they walked off Justin looked over at Cain. "Yoooo, you could've texted a brother and said that Sonya was gon' be here with Lauren."

"Hell, they just walked in right before you got here."

Justin frowned. "What brings Lauren out to the strip club? I mean, I know she likes to party, but I've never seen her at a strip club, let alone accompanying you."

Cain shrugged his shoulders. "I don't know. I told her that I was meeting you here and I thought that was it. Well, until I got in here, and she messaged me and asked if I would be okay with her coming too."

"Damn, she feeling good."

Cain nodded to agree. "Too damn good, but hey who am I to stop my lady from coming to a strip club with me? Hell, let's both have some fun. She don't seem like she's against any of it. She's been dropping mo' one's than me in this bitch."

Justin grinned.

"I ain't lying." Cain laughed. "I love it."

"I bet you do." Justin said. "But, damn I wish I knew Sonya was here. I might've changed my mind 'bout coming."

"Don't get scared now. I told you the girl was a lil crazy before you fucked her."

"How do you tell a bitch no when she sucks dick like pro?"

Cain shrugged. "You got a point my dirty."

"Plus, shawty got a whole husband at home. I don't know why she was stalking me like that."

"It was the dick." Cain uttered, "Nothing but the dick."

"You right because apparently her husband wasn't fucking her good. I gave her the D and she went straight crazy on me."

"Loco," Cain slid in.

"Shawty was poppin' up at my job and shit like she ain't married. I had to tell her to chill out. Then she threatening to leave her husband. Shit, I told her she better stay with that man because I wasn't gon' be with her. She fine and cute, but I ain't want her like that. I'm used to decent pussy. It's that rare gushy shit I be crazy 'bout."

Cain laughed, "Bruuuuuh."

"Nah, I'm for real." Justin clowned. "You remember when I was at y'all house and she popped up there trying to go off on me because I wasn't returning her calls? I thought the bitch had lost her mind. Hell, I stopped over because of her. I didn't wanna run into her crazy ass. She even called me one night talking about, she was going to tell her husband about me. Man, I hung up in that bitch face."

Cain laughed out loud. "Yea, shawty was doing too much."

"Now, she in here speaking like we good. Hell nawl, we ain't good. Shit, I ain't gon' lie I'm kinda scared of the broad. I don't know what she'll do next." He said, just as a half-naked waitress walked over and served them drinks.

"Well, it's been about 6 months since y'all fucked around. Hopefully, she's over it now."

"Yea, I hope so because if she's thinking I'll ever fuck with her again, she's sadly mistaken."

Cain bobbed his head to the music, as the stripper bounced her jiggly ass in front of him. He sipped from his clear, plastic cup. "Damn Bruh," he grinned, but cut his laughter short as he noticed some familiar faces walking into the VIP section next to them. "What are the fucking odds of this shit happening?"

Justin wasn't paying any attention until he followed his brother's surprised eyes to the section next to them. He spotted Sofia and a few of her friends. "That's yo' baby mama ain't it?"

"Hell yea!" Cain responded with an unpleasant look.

"Wow, this some crazy shit."

"Real crazy with Lauren being in this bitch, too. I hope she don't think I knew nothing about Sofia being here tonight."

"Well, she shouldn't think like that. If that was the case you wouldn't have wanted her to come when she asked." Justin smiled, as he threw ones on the stripper bent over in front of them making her ass clap.

"That's true, but you know how women are." Cain said.

"You're right. They can be unpredictable at times."

Justin agreed. "What they got going on, anyway? They celebrating something with all them white and pink balloons. Shawty right there got a cake in her hand."

"Yea, I peeped that."

"Everybody in her circle dressed in white. They wildn' over there too."

"I just hope Sofia don't see me." Cain said, just as he and Sofia locked eyes. He tried to quickly look away like he'd been watching the stripper the whole time.

She smiled while throwing up her hand and loudly speaking. "Hey baby daddy," Sofia called out, the minute she spotted Cain.

"Ah shit," Justin uttered.

"Damn," Cain whispered, as he politely spoke back. "Wassup Sofia?" He said, feeling annoyed at just the fact that she was there. However, he couldn't help but notice how sexy she looked while admiring her tasteful sense of style. For once she was casually dressed in a simple white, one-piece romper that was mid-thigh length and hung off her shoulders. She had on a pair of white sandals to match. Her hair was pulled up in a ball right on the top of her head. It was the first time he'd ever saw her without a colorful wig on her head. She actually looked like a decent girl, not just some random, cute hood rat.

"She got some baddies with her too."

"I see." Cain agreed.

"Damn, I think I'm gon' ease on over in their section. I'd rather give my money to them." He joked.

"Nah, you need to chill out with me. I thought you had a woman now, anyway."

"Who Shyla?"

"Yea, Cashmere's homegirl."

"She's cool. I definitely like her, but we ain't locked it in yet. I wouldn't mind if we do but I ain't gon' rush it. She got a few things going on right now, so I'm being patient."

"I feel you," he said, just as Sofia walked up.

"Wassup Baby Daddy? I didn't expect to see you here."

Damn, she would walk over here. Cain thought, but then responded with an unbothered look on his face. "I didn't expect to see you here either."

"What y'all got going on over there?" Justin butted in.

"It's my sister's birthday, so I was throwing her a lil some, some."

"Talking 'bout YoYo?" Cain asked.

"Yea, but she ain't made it here yet. She promised she'd come even though this ain't her type of party, but I'm gon' need her to loosen up a bit." Sofia grinned.

"Well, you look nice." Cain said, as he glanced around to make sure that Lauren wasn't close by.

"Thanks Baby Daddy," Sofia smiled.

"Where's my boy at anyway?"

"Oh, mama got him tonight. She too wants YoYo to get a life." She laughed. "You coming to see him tomorrow?"

"Yea, I'll stop by for a little while." He answered.

By: Tiece

"Okay, well y'all have fun." She said, as she turned to leave out of their section. She and Lauren nearly bumped right into each other. "Oh, uh excuse me." Sofia politely said. "How are you?"

Lauren apprehensively smiled, but definitely wasn't expecting to see the baby mama there. "Hey, I'm good and you?"

"I'm good." Sofia said with a smile and then walked off.

Lauren looked over at Cain with an unsure expression. "What is she doing here?"

"She said she's here to celebrate her sister's birthday." Cain explained, as Lauren sat down next to him.

"Oh okay," Lauren responded. She was feeling too good to let that bother her. "Want some honey lemon-pepper wings?"

"Nah Bae, I'm good." Cain responded. He glanced over beside him to see that Justin was now being entertained by Sonya.

"So, can we link later tonight?" Sonya asked, while smiling in Justin's face.

"Nah, shawty I'm good." He responded, while turning up his drink.

"You sure? My lips really miss your dick. Both sets," she added with a seductive smile.

"Oh yea?" He grinned. "Well, I'm gon' have to pass tonight." He said, while standing to his feet. "My bitch over there." He said, looking towards Sofia's section.

"Oh, I didn't know that. Which one is her?" Sonya asked, as Justin stood to his feet.

Fallin' In Love With The Goat 3

"The one in the white," he answered, and then smoothly walked off leaving Sonya with my mouth partly open. He didn't know which bitch he was talking about, but he was going to mingle with all of them. He would do whatever it took to get Sonya off his back.

Jabari sat in his car parked outside of Club 2, he couldn't sit one more minute in his house thinking. The circumstances surrounding his emotional state were way more than he thought he could handle. The best thing was for him to shower, get dressed and get out of the house to clear his mind. If nothing else, a fat ass dropping it like it was hot on top of a grinding lap dance should do the trick. All he needed was to shake the ill feelings that were plaguing his mind about Cashmere.

He glanced down at his cell phone, still noticing that Cashmere hadn't responded to his message. He didn't know if that was proving her guilt or if she was purposely ignoring him but either way it had pissed him off. The last thing he wanted to do was get caught in something he should've left alone in the first place. "Damn," he whispered just as his phone alerted him of an incoming text message. He glanced down to see who it was and then read it.

Hey you. Ashley's father did pick her up not long ago, so she's gone for the night. I'd like you to consider an invite if you come out the house later tonight. TIANA

Hey Beautiful. I just might do that. I'll let you know in a couple of hours. JAH

Okay cool. TIANA

Jabari smiled, as he turned up his flask filled with straight Hennessey. Tiana definitely had a way of making him feel better. A frown quickly appeared on his face just as he noticed Bruno and Melissa walking into the club.

They seem to be very happy as of lately. He pondered to himself. He also saw Tonio walking in not ten minutes behind them with a woman on his arm. *What's tonight, ladies night at the strip?* He thought, as he pulled his blunt from behind his ear and then lit it. As he sat there toking memories of Slick crossed his mind. Any other time, he'd be sitting right next to him clowning around and joking about something funny. A part of him felt lost without him, then another part felt angry and pissed. He sighed while inhaling the good shit and letting go of the bad. Somehow he had to find a way to get past this unbelievable nightmare that was already haunting his every emotion. *What the fuck?* He thought with a shake of the head. But a familiar face caught his attention and changed his entire mood.

Quickly, he let down his window. "Ayyyyyee, shawty with the white dress on." he called out.

Yolanda turned to face him with a cute smile on her face. "Heeeyyy," she sang while waving her hand in the air."

"Come here with yo' sexy self."

Yolanda blushed, while making her way over to Jabari's car. "Wassup handsome? We meet again."

"I'm surprised it's here," Jabari responded, while admiring her look. She was beautiful standing before him in a mid-thigh length, white fitted dress and a pair of white Red Bottom heels on. She had her hair pulled up in a bun and was looking rather seductive, even more with her tattoos visibly showing a bad girl image, as he stared at her. "Damn, you're looking tasty tonight." He told her, then turning up his flask filled with straight Hennessy.

"I'll take that as a compliment."

"You better," he teased, but was dead serious.

"You look like you're about lit yourself." She smiled, as he turned up the flask again, followed by taking a pull from his blunt.

"A lil bit." He responded. "What brings you here?"

"My sister is having a lil party for me."

"A party? It's yo' birthday or something?"

Yolanda nodded her head with a smile. "Yea, it's my birthday."

"Well damn, happy birthday," Jabari told her. "I guess this would be a dope place to celebrate it."

"My sister thinks I need to unwind a bit. My mom agrees, so she's the babysitter for the night."

Jabari laughed. "You got it that bad?"

"Yea, maybe," she grinned.

"Come on, get in. Unless you gotta get to your people."

"They'll be alright." Yolanda teased and then wasted no time getting in the car on the passenger side.

Jabari looked over at her. His eyes went from her pretty face, down to her smooth legs, then to her light pink polished toenails. He stared back in her eyes, puffing the blunt. "You smoke?"

Yolanda shook her head. "Yea, but I only smoke CBD joints."

Jabari frowned. "CBD joints?"

By: Tiece

Yolanda grinned. "Yea, the pre-rolled ones that be in the Vape stores. I get mine out the mall though. They're the real deal."

Jabari laughed. "So, you smoke CBD which is weed without the THC—"

"Right."

"And they roll it in joint papers and sell it in the vape stores?"

"Yea," Yolanda answered, while giggling. "You make it sound bad."

"Nah, I ain't say that. It's just interesting that you've never tried the good stuff. Anyway, it's your birthday, you wanna hit the real deal?" he mocked.

Yolanda shook her head. "Nah, I'll pass." She said.

"A'ight, no pressure. I always offer, so you don't feel left out."

"I appreciate the offer," she said, but then paused like she was thinking about something. "I think I'm gonna hit that. Shit, it's my birthday and you only live once."

Jabari grinned. "YOLO," he clowned, causing Yolanda to laugh out loud. "You sure you wanna hit this? But hold up, this is ain't that bullshit you used to."

"You're scaring me."

"Don't get scared now." Jabari joked as they laughed.

"Okay, Okay, blow some smoke in my face. That might be all I need, or shall I say can handle."

"Come here, I'll give you a light shotgun." He told her, while thinking it had been 10 plus years since he had given somebody a shotgun. "When I blow the smoke in your face you inhale. Don't take inhale too deep, just do it softly." He coached. "I don't wanna blow yo' mind and have you too high."

Yolanda blushed. "Okaaaay," she sang, as Jabari put the fired end of the blunt in his mouth. He cupped his hands between his mouth and Yolanda's mouth, as to keep in as much smoke as possible. He then lightly blew the smoke in her face. She inhaled, but quickly started coughing.

"I told you not to inhale too hard."

"I didn't think it was going to be that much smoke." She said through coughs.

"You gon' be high as hell." He laughed.

"I knooow." She playfully hit him on the leg.

"If you don't mind me asking, how old are you?"

"I turned 32 years old."

"You're older than me, but only by a couple of months." He told her.

"So, you have a birthday coming up in about two months?"

"Yep," Jabari told her. "November 20th."

"You're a Scorpio."

"Yep," he said again, while looking over at her and sipping from his flask. "What?" he asked as she smiled.

"Nothing," she responded, with a shake of the head.

"It's something for you to be smiling like that. Is it because I said I was a Scorpio?"

"Maybe," she answered. "I heard that Scorpios were born from the Sex Goddess."

Jabari laughed out loud, but nodded his head to agree. "Those are facts."

"I knew you were going to say that." She grinned, as her phone chirped of an incoming text message. She opened the message to read it.

Where are you? You better not be flaking on us tonight." SOFIA

I'm outside. I'll be in shortly. YOYO

Once she finished her text, she looked in Jabari's direction. "My sister is looking for me now."

"Well, let's go in and celebrate your birthday, Miss Yoyo." Jabari teased.

"You're funny. I just updated my signature to that." She grinned. "I'm high as hell. You ready?"

"'Bout as ready as I'll get." He responded, but just as he was getting ready to get out the car, Yolanda softly grabbed him by his face. As their eyes met, so did their lips. Yolanda passionately kissed him, and then when it was over she blushed with a lighthearted chuckle.

"Just in case I forget to tell you later, I just wanted you to know that I had a really good time tonight. Chilling with you has made my birthday a special one."

Jabari shot a handsome smile her way with a satisfied nod. "The pleasure's all mine."

Chapter Five

"How was Club 2 last night? Did you have fun?" Tiana asked.

"I had so much fun." Lauren answered.

"I still can't believe you went. I mean, I know you like to party, but you never cared for the strip club."

"I know, but it's actually not a bad spot to parlay. Hell, me and Sonya was wildin'. I know Cain was just as shocked to see me let go and enjoy myself. He was probably more surprised than you were to know I was going."

"I bet, because I was shocked as hell." Tiana agreed. "You'll party, but you're not that open minded when it comes to certain things."

"Well, my mind is wide open now."

"I see." Tiana responded with a shake of the head. "So, who all was there?"

"Justin came—"

"Hold up, Justin and Sonya was in the same place? How did that work out?"

"It really didn't. Justin didn't pay her ass no attention. I tried to tell her that she was doing too much back when they were kicking it, but she didn't want to listen."

"She definitely went overboard. I don't know what he did to her ass, but she was gone."

By: Tiece

"Gone ain't the word." Lauren uttered.

"She still with her husband?"

"Chile, that man ain't going nowhere. I don't know what she did to him, but his ass is gone too."

Tiana laughed out loud. "Apparently, because she be running circles around his ass."

"On top of that, she's still in love with Justin. She kept watching him last night."

"What he was doing?"

"Over there entertaining Cain's baby mama and her girls."

Tiana frowned. "You didn't tell me that his baby mama was there too. Which one?"

"Which one you think? The one that seems to always be around."

"The lil young one?"

"Yea, Sofia." Lauren responded.

"Shit, how did that go?"

"She stayed in her lane and I stayed in mine. So did Cain because he knew not to cross the gun line."

Tiana laughed. "Not the gun line."

Lauren grinned with a nod of the head.

"I see you bought some of that wine."

"I got me 5 bottles the next day after I left your house."

"Damn, 5 whole bottles?"

"Yep, 5 whole bottles." She laughed. "You want some?"

"Damn right I want some." Tiana smiled.

Lauren got 2 glasses and started pouring her and Tiana a drink. "So, Jabari was there last night too."

"Oh, was he?"

"Yep, I thought you knew. He didn't tell you?"

"Well, not exactly. He did say that he would hit me up and let me know if he was coming through, but he never did."

"That's probably because he was too busy entertaining Sofia's sister."

Tiana frowned. "Talking about the redbone chick that was with her at the track?"

"Yep, her." Lauren answered.

"Oh, what kind of entertaining? Do tell little sister."

"Well, they walked in together for starts. He came over where we were, but he didn't stay long."

"What you mean by that?" Tiana pondered.

"Well, Sofia was throwing her sister a birthday shindig in the VIP section next to ours. That's pretty much where Jabari and Justin hung out at. I know why Justin was over there—"

"Yea, he was trying to stay away from Sonya I'm sure."

"Pretty much," Lauren agreed. "Jabari was just chilling mostly, but Sofia's sister was definitely all up on him. He didn't seem to pressed to back her ass up either."

By: Tiece

"Well, I guess it's not much that I can say, being that we're not exactly exclusive. So, he can do whatever he wants to do. I just wish I would've come out last night too now. I didn't because I was hoping that he was coming over."

"He would've been shocked to see you walking up in there." Lauren told her, as she sipped from her glass of wine.

"I bet he would've been. But, hey, it's all good."

"Well, I think you should know that they walked out together when the club closed. Jabari did get in his car alone, and so did she. No telling what they did after that. I know she was lit and he was feeling pretty good too."

"Maybe he went home and slept it off. I haven't talked to him this morning yet. I'll probably message him later if he don't message me sooner." She said, now sipping from her glass of wine.

"So, do you see yourself being with Jabari?"

Tiana shrugged. "It sounds good and it looks even better, but I don't know. Jabari has a lot going on. Plus, Cashmere is pregnant, and I know he wants to be there for his baby. So, I really can't call it. I know one thing; I'm not gonna get my hopes up or go all out for a nigga that ain't going all in with me. That's for sure."

"Shit, I feel you Sis. Relationships are the worse nowadays."

"And, being single is a close second." Tiana chimed in. "Honestly, I like being single. I don't have any expectations. I rather enjoy sleeping alone at night. I don't have to look out for nobody but Ashley. I control the remote control and can very well watch whatever the hell I wanna watch. It's lonely sometimes, but for the most part I'm handling this single life pretty well for myself."

"I totally understand, although I've never really lived the single life. It is times when I wished I knew that feeling."

Yea, but you and Cain always weather the storm."

"But at what cost?" Lauren pondered while sipping her drink. "Sometimes, I just wanna leave him and not look back."

"Is it because of the cheating?"

"Of course." Lauren answered. "And, other things—"

"Such as," Tiana pondered while sipping her wine.

"Him feeling like he runs things and without him I'd be lost."

"Does he say that?"

"No, but I know what he's thinking."

"I don't know, Sis. You might just be overthinking that part. I've known Cain for a long time and he's never been the type. He takes very good care of you. I mean, shit look at the way you live. For me to be the oldest, I've always envied what y'all had."

"Really?" Lauren asked, now not feeling so bad.

"Yea," Tiana responded. "No relationship is perfect. No man or woman is perfect, but if he shows you that he's a changed man then you should go with that. You could get with somebody else and it could be much, much worse than what you have now."

"You're right." Lauren said. "I'm not leaving my man for these scrubs to jump on him and take what I got."

"There you go. That's the Sister I know." Tiana said.

"And, you shouldn't let another bitch scroll in and distract Jabari either. You're slipping Sis."

"Fine time for you tell me that. You should've told me last night what was going on at the club."

"Yea, but after you said you weren't coming out, I figured there was no need."

"Yea, but if your ass hit me up and said that then I would've gotten my black ass up and been at Club 2 last night."

"I'm sorry Sis. I was fucked up. I peeped it but at the same time I was just thinking that I'd keep an eye on him."

"Fine job of doing that. Seems he was still enjoying himself while you watched."

"Well, it wasn't exactly like that. He was mostly cooling, even though she was the one all over him."

"Don't tell me that. I'm starting to feel a lil jealous." Tiana admitted, as she held out her glass for more wine. "Damn, it' ain't even noon and we're already getting lit."

"It's drink o'clock somewhere."

Tiana laughed, as Lauren's cell phone rang.

"I don't know this number."

"Probably a damn telemarketer."

"I know better. They better not be calling me on a fucking Sunday." Lauren fussed. "HELLO."

"Um, hello," the soft-spoken voice said on the other end.

"Yes, hello." Lauren said, with a sarcastic, very bothered sounding tone.

"Hey, this Hazel, Neveah's mom. Is this Lauren?"

Fallin' In Love With The Goat 3

Lauren's eyes widened. "Yes it is." She responded. Immediately her tone calmed down a few notches. "So, what do I owe the pleasure of this call?"

"Who is that?" Tiana whispered in the background.

Lauren held up her finger, as eased into the nearby dining room for a bit of privacy.

"First let me say that I got your number from Cain, not long ago."

"Okay," Lauren said, being that Cain didn't even give her a heads up that his baby mama would be calling her.

"I hope you don't mind."

"No, you're fine."

"I wanted to know if we could sit down and talk about Nevaeh spending time with her father at y'all's house."

"You think we need to talk about that or you and Cain?" Lauren asked.

"Well, Cain and I have talked about it, many times at that. Now, I think it's only right that we talk. If I allow him to take my baby home with him then she'll be around you, is that correct."

"Yea."

"So, I think it's only right that you and I sit down and talk."

"Okay."

"Look, I'm not trying to make this difficult, but my daughter is only 2 years old. She has never spent time with Cain, other than him being around me or my mom. He has been trying to come around her more. She's actually been warming up to him faster than I thought. So, he asked me if he could take her with him that way he could spend more time with her, instead of having to sit over my place."

"Well, I appreciate you calling to speak with me about it." Lauren said. "I would really love for Cain to be able to spend time with his babies' home. So, yes, let's definitely sit down and talk."

"Okay, great. Are you available on Friday? I work all week and when I'm off I have my baby to tend to. But Friday, I get off at noon."

"Noon works for me." Lauren said.

"Okay, I'll see you then."

"Okay, bye." Lauren said, as she headed back into the kitchen area where her sister was sitting.

"Who was that?" Tiana anxiously pondered.

"Hazel."

Tiana frowned.

"Cain's other baby mama."

"Noooo, what she wanted?"

"She want us to sit down and talk. I guess about her daughter coming over here."

"Well, that was big of her." Tiana said.

"I hope that it goes well," Lauren said. "My only problem is that Cain didn't give me a heads up that she was calling. If he felt comfortable giving her my number, he should've felt comfortable to let me know."

Fallin' In Love With The Goat 3

"I agree."

"Anyway, I gotta pee. Hold tight and we can run to the grocery store to grab some meat for the grill when I return."

"Sounds like a plan to me." Tiana said, as Lauren disappeared down the hall. Tiana sat tapping her fingers lightly on the glass top table. Thoughts of Jabari crossed her mind. After anxiously waiting to hit him up, she grabbed her cell phone.

Good Morning Handsome. What you doing? TIANA

A few minutes went by and then Jabari responded back.

Good Morning Beautiful. I'm just waking up. Wyd? JAH

Just drinking a lil wine with my sister before going to the grocery store. We're cooking on the grill today. You should come over to your brother's house. TIANA

Cool, I'll do that. JAH

Great. I'll see you later. TIANA

That's the plan. See you later. JAH

Tiana took another sip of wine and the only thoughts floating through her mind was making sure that she continued to play her role and stay in her lane when it came to Jabari. She couldn't imagine falling in love completely and then getting her heart broken. She'd protected it for a long time and letting her guard down was not something she was ready to do. However, if Jabari's actions matched those of wanting to be with her then maybe she'd consider letting him in her heart.

By: Tiece

Jabari sat up on the side of the bed. He stretched his arms out, and then glanced out the window. The neighborhood view was peaceful and very suburban 'ish. Jabari leaned down and grabbed his fresh white Air Force One's and put them on his feet. He had slept with his jeans and his shirt on. Normally, that would've been a very uncomfortable way of sleeping, but it actually made sense with how the night ended. Plus, he still got in a few hours of undisturbed sleep.

He looked up with a smile on his face.

"Hey Boo," Yolanda said, as she walked out of the master bathroom. She shook her head still feeling embarrassed at how the night ended.

"You good, because when you fell asleep you was out for the count." Jabari grinned.

"Damn, I know. I don't know what happened. All I know is that the room was spinning but I didn't want to throw up."

"You was feeling good."

"I know, and I haven't had that much fun in a long time. That was the first time I smoked weed and I really enjoyed it. It's not something I wanna make a habit of, but it was definitely the main thing that mellowed me out. That and the Hennessey shots," she added.

"Right, because you had started throwing them back too, one shot after the other."

"Don't make me shame."

Jabari grinned. "I could tell you don't get out and have fun much. That's all the women kept saying to you."

Fallin' In Love With The Goat 3

Yolanda shook her head. "They ain't have to pick at me like that."

"Yea, they were relentless."

"Well, I wanna thank you for following me home and making sure that I got here safely. You made sure I got in the bed, practically tucked me in and you stayed even though you kept saying you had to go."

"That's because you kept asking me to. I counted the times and it was about a million."

Yolanda laughed out loud. "You tripping this morning."

"Nah, but you could very well hold your own, though. You didn't swerve not one time on the way here; but maybe that's because you were only going about 25 miles per hour."

"You got jokes, huh?"

"Nah," Jabari laughed. "But it's the truth."

Yolanda walked over and then sat down on the bed beside Jabari. "You're a real gentleman. You don't run across those anymore and I appreciate you."

Jabari shrugged his shoulders. "It's all good. You're good." He said, while standing to his feet. "It's been fun and all, but I have a busy day today."

"I totally understand. I'll walk you out." She said, standing up to lead Jabari out. They walked out in the hallway.

"You have a nice, big house. Why your sister just won't come live with you here? You have more than enough room."

By: Tiece

Yolanda shook her head. "Unt-unt, my sister and I get along great when we're living a part. The minute we attempt to live together, all hell breaks loose."

Jabari laughed, as he followed Yolanda down the stairs. "I know how that it." He uttered.

Once they made it down the stairs, through the living room and then stopped in the open foyer that led to the front door, Yolanda stopped to look back at him. "So, are you in a relationship?"

"Well, I'm single but I ain't gon' lie. I'm kinda seeing somebody."

"Kinda?"

"Yea, kinda," he answered. "We kick it, but we ain't made it official. I don't even think I'm ready for that yet." He said, not wanting to get into the fact that he'd just gotten out of a relationship with Cashmere and she had practically turned him against getting seriously involved with somebody else."

"Well, maybe we can get to know each other a lot better? That's if you're down."

Jabari smiled. "I don't see nothing wrong with that." He answered, as he pulled Yolanda in for a hug. She smelled good from the shower she had just taken, as her hair still dripped a bit from her washing it. "What's the plans for today?"

"My mom and my siblings are throwing me a birthday kickback today. So, I'll be there most of the day. You're welcome to come through if you want."

"I appreciate the invite, but I've made plans already for the day."

"That's cool. I hope to see you soon though."

Fallin' In Love With The Goat 3

"You will." Jabari said with a smile. "Oh, you will." With that he swiftly made his way out to his car which was parked in the driveway. He got in still smiling. It was something about Yolanda that he was feeling, but still he had a lot going on.

Thoughts of Cashmere crossed his mind, as he glanced down at his cell phone. Still no word from her. The message he sent clearly showed that she had read it. "I don't know why she keeps playing with me," he said while pressing the ignition button to start the car. Before backing out, he decided to send her another message.

I guess you not responding means it's some truth to the message I sent you. JAH

Within seconds, she was responding back.

Or it could mean that I don't have time for your absurd innuendos. Again, my main concern is my baby. Whether he's yours or not, one thing for sure is that he's mine. So, I'm not sure where you got that information from, but you can follow it up all you want. Cashmere ain't got time. CASHMERE

Jabari shook his head once reading it, but before he could respond she had messaged back.

And again, I'm very sorry for what I did. It was never my intention to hurt you. I did some very selfish things. I'm embarrassed, sad, hurt and angry with myself for going there. I know you're not in the head space of forgiving me and I totally understand. However, some day I hope to make up for my dishonesty and betrayal. I can't say I'm sorry enough. CASHMERE

"Wow," Jabari uttered. "This woman is hell. Boy, she's hell."

By: Tiece

Chapter Six

Cashmere pulled up to her mother's house and parked her car out front in the driveway. She glanced back in the rearview mirror, noticing an unfamiliar car parked by the curbstone. She hunched her shoulders, not thinking anything of it, while at the same time hoping that she wasn't walking in on her mother's extracurricular activities. The thought alone made her gag inside. Before getting out, her cell phone rang as she looked down at the caller ID display. It was Shyla calling. Without hesitation, she answered the call.

"Hey Bestie."

"Hey my fat, fat." Shyla mocked. "Somebody turned 19 weeks today. I think it's my little bun in your oven."

Cashmere grinned. "Girl, time is really flying."

"I'm tryna to tell you." Shyla agreed.

"Two months ago, we were having Skylar's birthday celebration, now tomorrow, we'll be celebrating my baby's gender reveal."

"I knooooow, and I'm so excited about it."

"I don't know why you're so excited. You're the one that knows his gender."

"Well, I think that's only fair since I am the God-Mommy and how do you know it's a him."

Cashmere shrugged with a smirk. "I'm just saying."

"Okay, just saying." Shyla teased. "Are you going to send Jabari an invite?"

"Of course, I am. He might be still acting crazy, half talking to me and shit, but it's cool. I can understand him being in his feelings. Technically, two months really isn't a lot of time to get over something as devastating as I put him through. So, I just do my part from afar. When I went in for my 14-week check-up I told him. If he wanted to come he could've. He didn't show and that was cool with me. But, I sent him pictures of the sonograms, even though his lil butt wasn't positioned to tell us the gender."

"You really think it's a boy, but I'm not telling."

"You ain't got to. I already know." Cashmere joked but was very serious. "Anyways, I also sent him the sonogram pictures from yesterday's visit. I only sent the ones without his penis showing."

Shyla laughed. "You need to stop."

"Well, I figured if he wants to know the gender he'll come to the reveal party and find out just like me."

"I feel you. What does Jabari want? I mean, have y'all discussed if he wanted a boy or a girl?"

"A girl. He wants a girl. I don't know if he's still as excited about the baby as I am, but from his actions, I doubt it." Cashmere admitted.

"Awww, I pray for y'all. I pray that he comes around someday soon, because I know your heart and I know you really want him to be the baby's father."

"He is." Cashmere said.

"That's right girl. Keep speaking it into existence."

Cashmere grinned. "Bitch whatever," she teased and then added. "But let's not get off the subject here. How long are you going to let Rich dictate what you do or don't do in your life? The nigga has a whole nother woman and a baby. I've never saw you as the person to take no shit from nan nigga; especially not to this extent."

"You already know why I've been holding back with Justin. I don't want him going to jail for whooping Rich's ass. The only reason why I haven't called the police on his ass is because of the kids."

"It's been over a month though Shy. You gotta put a stop to his ass. Let Justin rough the nigga up. That'll stop him from hanging out in front of your house and being nosey. He's either on some borderline stalking shit or he's just doing this shit to intimidate you because he knows your heart. And, I put my money on the latter. Rich doesn't want you to move on because he knows what he got—"

"Had," Shyla cut in.

"Seems like he still got it because yo' ass won't move on. I really think it's time for you to move on. Show him what time it is. Who cares if he pops up to your house acting weird? You shouldn't. Either call the police or let Justin whoop his ass."

"Justin is probably tired of playing games with me by now. We don't even talk on a regular like we used to. I'm starting to think that maybe it's just me. I work a lot and I'm doing the best I can to maintain now that I know it's over between me and Rich. I just never seen a man that is hell bent on living the way he wants to but doesn't want me to move on."

Fallin' In Love With The Goat 3

"Girl, all men are like that. They want their cakes and eat it too and I ain't talking about just one damn cake.

These muthafuckas want the whole damn bakery."

Shyla laughed. "I guess you're right."

"I know I'm right."

"Anyway, what you doing?"

"Just pulled up to Jeanie's house."

Shyla laughed. "Just say to your mama's house."

"I did," Cashmere chuckled.

"It still sounds funny when you call her Jeanie. You never called her that growing up. It wasn't until Earl entered the picture."

"Unt-unt," Cashmere said with a shake of the head. "You get serious too damn fast and I ain't with it. I don't care to talk about Earl and I'm perfectly fine with calling mama by her government name. It's not that serious. You better focus on your own shit because I have a gut feeling that you're going to let a good man slip right out of your hands and that's because you're too afraid to put your foot down. Hell, I don't see why you're scared anyway. You got Rich by the balls. You better start playing those cards in your favor."

"You're right." Shyla agreed. She was definitely taking Cashmere's advice to heart. "Well, tell Auntie I said hey and call me later when you're free. I still have a few more things to get for the gender reveal."

"I can't wait. I'm getting more and more excited about it."

"You should be." Shyla said. "Love ya chick."

By: Tiece

"Love ya back." Cashmere responded, and with that they ended their call.

Cashmere got out of the car and headed up the steps that led to her mother's front door. With one ring of the doorbell, Jeanie was opening the door.

"Hey Cash," she said with a pleasant smile. "Come on in."

"Hey Jeanie." Cashmere spoke back.

"So, I'm still Jeanie I see."

"Well, hey mama."

Jeanie smiled. "Much better."

"So, how are you? I haven't seen you in a while."

"Almost a year." Jeanie cut in.

Cashmere shook her head with a slick roll of the eyes. "It has not been a year, maybe 6 or 8 months."

"Like I said, a year," Jeanie reiterated, but quickly changed the subject. "You're so beautiful and already showing. How far along are you?"

"I'll be 5 months on tomorrow." She said while going inside of her purse. She came out with an invitation to her gender reveal. "Here, I would like for you to come."

Jeanie smiled, as she reached for the invitation. On the front of the envelope it read, Cashmere's gender reveal. "When did this start?"

"What?"

Fallin' In Love With The Goat 3

"Gender reveal parties," Jeanie answered. "Back in our day we either found out during a sonogram, performed old rituals, or just waited until we had the baby."

"Gender parties is the new thing now. People have some really nice ones too. You're so outdated and out of touch with reality."

"I try to keep up. It's just some stuff I'm unaware of, simply because I'm not around it. That's just like social media. I just got me a Facebook page. I figured it was time for me to see what the hype is about."

"As long as you don't be stalking my page or picking up no men; particularly young men."

"You don't have to worry. I have no plans of using Facebook to attract men. I can simply meet them in the clubs. And, I won't be stalking you either. Your auntie stalks you and Shyla's page, but I ain't got time."

"Sit down somewhere," Cashmere uttered, as she sat down on the couch across from the TV."

"So, do you think you'll be able to come? I know it's last minute." She asked as Jeanie pulled the invitation out of the envelope. She smiled as she looked it over.

"Yes, I wouldn't miss this for the world. Plus, Net had already told me about it. I was just waiting to see if I'd get an invite. I know you call every now and then, but it's not the same as you stopping by. I miss that."

Cashmere smiled. All she ever wanted was a better relationship with her mother. Even though she felt betrayed by her actions, Cashmere also accepted a lot of the blame.

By: Tiece

"I see Shyla is the hostess and the what?" Jeanie asked while squinting at the card. "Oh, the God-Mommy?"

Cashmere laughed. "Yea, she's the God-Mother, we just call it the God-Mommy."

"That's cute. I love the theme. Is it a Prince or a Princess?"

"Yes, Shy is going all out. I can't wait until I see it all come together."

"So, it's at her house?"

"Yes, it's going to be in her backyard. You know she has a huge screened-in porch with a patio connected to it. So, it'll be lots of space for the activities she has planned."

Jeanie smiled. "We haven't had a family gathering in a long time. I'm really looking forward to this."

Cashmere smiled back. "Me too."

"So, Shyla knows the gender?"

"Yes, but I do too."

Jeanie frowned. "So, you know too?"

"I didn't technically see the sonogram nor have Shyla told me, but I do believe it's a boy."

"I would love to have a grandson." Jeanie said, as she stood up to fix her a glass of liquor. She walked over to the bar, still smiling and then poured a shot of Jack Daniels. "But, that's just something you're saying right? That's not something you're sure of?"

Cashmere shrugged. "I'm not 100% sure, but I'm sure."

Fallin' In Love With The Goat 3

Jeanie playfully rolled her eyes. "So, just say you don't know but you hope it's a boy."

"Hush mama." Cashmere grinned. "You good?" she asked with a concerned expression. She knew Jeanie would have a drink from time to time, but something was definitely off about her demeanor. She seemed nervous and fidgety and even though she was being pleasantly nice, her odd behavior stood out.

"Yea, I'm good." Jeanie told her.

"How's counseling? Auntie told me you had started going about a month ago."

"Yes, I'm actually 35 days clean. I haven't taken any pills since before then. All I do is have a lil alcohol here or there." Jeanie explained.

"You don't think that'll make you want to get higher or shall I say a different high that could lead you back to the pills?"

"No, I'm good. I'm still going to counseling and from the looks of things I'll be doing that for a long time. I wanna do better by you and definitely by my grand baby. I feel like I have a second chance."

"I'm glad to hear that." Cashmere said.

"You want something to drink? Some tea, water, Kool-aide?"

"No, I'm not staying long. I just wanted to make sure you got your invitation from me and nobody else."

"I do appreciate it." Jeanie said, and then decided to stick her nose where it didn't belong. "So, Net told me about your situation."

Cashmere frowned. "What situation?"

"You know, the paternity situation."

"I don't know who talk more, Auntie or her big mouth daughter."

Jeanie laughed, but then turned serious again. "Are you good though? Does Jabari plan on being there for you? Has he been there for you?" she asked all in one breath.

"I'm good and to answer your other question, Jabari is doing what he needs to do, nothing more or less."

"Well, if it's not Jabari's at least you'll be able to get a social security check."

Cashmere frowned, as she stood to her feet. "I guess that's my queue to leave."

"No, don't rush off." Jeanie told her. Even though Cashmere was a bit offended, Jeanie didn't seem to think she had said anything wrong.

"No, I think I will. I'll see you at the gender reveal tomorrow."

"Okay, I'm looking forward to it." She reached out for a hug, as Cashmere apprehensively gave her what she wanted. It felt weird hugging her mother being that it had been so long since they were in that type of head space. The energy wasn't bad, but Cashmere knew when it was time to go.

"I'll talk to you later."

"Okay baby." Jeanie responded. She walked Cashmere out on the porch while watching her walk out to her car. She waved her hand in the air, until she was gone down the road and out of sight. She turned to walk back inside of her house. She sucked her teeth the minute she entered.

"Didn't I tell you to keep your ass in the bedroom?" Jeanie fussed.

"I wasn't about to let her see me. You act like I don't know how she feels about me." Earl said, as he reached into his pocket. "Sooooo, that's why you called me. Apparently, counseling ain't working."

"Cut to the chase. Do you have the pills or not?" Jeanie asked.

"Damn, slow down. Didn't I come over as soon as you called me?"

"Yea, and?"

"Well, it's been years since I've seen you. Chill for a minute. Let me take in this moment. I didn't think I would ever talk to you again. Hell, you don't even speak when I see you at the club."

"That's because we're not supposed to be in the same vicinity. I was told years ago to stay away from you. That was the one thing I told myself I'd do for my well-being, my sanity, and most importantly my daughter."

"Congratulations, you're doing a fine job at that." Earl teased. "I heard her say she's pregnant."

"Yes, and what's it to you?"

"Oh, nothing but somethings I guess never changes." He snuck in.

Jeanie frowned. "Meaning?"

"Well, you know with her being deceitful and shit."

"Earl, I'm telling you now—"

By: Tiece

"Okaaaay, damn you still feisty. Anyway, how does it feel to almost be a grandmother?"

"I'm proud to be a grandmother."

"Even though you still look like you're in your mid-twenties. I would never believe you're a grandmother."

"Thanks," Jeanie said. For a minute she even almost blushed.

"I'm sorry for the things I did. I wasn't well Jeanie."

"Look," Jeanie cut in. "I didn't call you here to go down memory lane or to talk about my daughter's business. I called you here because I was told from a friend of a friend that you're the man with the pills. I can pay for my shit, so don't think I want a handout. I just need to shop with somebody until my connect gets straight."

"I don't have no pills, Jeanie. The only thing I got is this white girl." He said, holding up the small plastic bag containing a white powdery substance.

Jeanie frowned. "Is that—"

"Cocaine," Earl chimed in. "It's the best shit on the streets right now."

"I don't do coke."

"You don't know what you do until you try it." Earl said, as he walked over to the sofa and sat down. He poured a line of the cocaine on the glass table in front of him and then looked over at Jeanie. "Just try it. If you don't like it go back to your pills."

"But, I was told you had the pills."

"Nah, I rarely have those, but what I do have will make you forget about the pills."

Fallin' In Love With The Goat 3

Jeanie looked over at him. She was definitely feigning for a really good high. The pills gave her a euphoric feeling, it heightened her senses, and allowed her to have the calmest of moods. She loved them more than anything else she tried. Cocaine was a drug she had yet to try and with good reason. It literally scared the shit out of her. The last thing she wanted to do was get hooked on that; especially already having a hard-enough time ditching the pills.

"This was the worst idea I could've ever come up with. I should've never called you."

"But you did. You said your connect was out, so why not shop with me?"

"Because you're a low-down muthafucka that slept with my daughter and then turned us against each other."

"Okaaay, just calm down Jeanie. We both were in some fucked up places in our lives back then. Plus, she started it!"

"Oh really?!" Jeanie spat with a shake of the head. "I can't believe you had the nerves to say that. I should've had your ass locked up back when I had the chance to."

"Don't talk like that. We had a good thing back then. I never should've allowed your daughter to seduce me."

Jeanie stared at Earl with menacing eyes. "I think it's time for you to go!" She yelled out, with an irritated tone. "I don't wanna do something that I'll regret."

Earl stood to his feet. "You called me over here. You did that because no matter what I did in the past you know I always had your back. Whatever you needed, I got it. Whatever you wanted, I provided. I may not have your choice of drug tonight, but I'll get it.

If you want pills I'll get those for you, and you won't even have to pay me for them."

"No, I don't think I want nothing from you." Jeanie said, as if she'd started coming back to her senses. "Please get out of my house!"

"Damn, you ain't gotta go bipolar on me. I'll leave, but you got my number if you need me. I'll leave this here though. You may change your mind later." Earl said, as he left the lines of powder on the glass table. As he got to the door to exit, he stopped to stare at Jeanie. "Damn, you still fine as hell. If only I had one more chance—"

"Go suck a dick!!!" Jeanie yelled, her facial expression told him that she really wanted to say more, but he had better been glad she didn't. "Earl, if you don't get the fuck outta my—"

"Okay, okaaaay," Earl dragged, as he headed out the front door. "You'll be back."

"In your dreams," Jeanie said. She slammed her screen door shut behind him and locked it. She watched him head out to his car and leave. Taking in a deep breath, she realized what she had almost stirred up. Had she allowed Earl back in her life all hell would've broken loose. The relationship with her and Cashmere would've been null and void, and that wasn't something she could risk. More importantly, she really wanted to be a great grandmother. But reality had a sneaky way of ruining things, as she found herself gazing at the powder on the table. She shook her head with uneasy thoughts, while coaching herself.

"Jeanie, you're stronger than that."

Chapter Seven

Jabari pulled into the driveway of Slick's mother's house. Had he known she was having her house repainted and the rooftop done, he would've waited. Nevertheless, he was there to see what she wanted. It was strange to be there knowing that Slick wasn't. For some reason, he had yet to stop by. It was something about it that simply broke his heart and that's why he chose to stay away. If it hadn't been for Tiny messaging him, he probably still wouldn't have come at least not as early.

He got out of the car and headed up to the front door, but before he could knock Tiny opened the door. She stepped out on the porch to join him.

"Hey Jabari."

"Wassup Tiny," he said. "You should've told me that these people were going to be here. I could've came another day."

"No, you're good. Auntie is just getting some work done and since I'm moving back here she's getting me my own space added on to the back of the house. That way I can help watch her and make sure she's straight."

"Well, that's nice of you."

"I figured that's the least I could do. But I really just wanted to holla at you before Aunt Trudy did. I know you really haven't said much to me since I messaged you about Cashmere. I hope you're not mad at me, but I felt the need to tell you."

"Would you have told me that if Slick was still here?"

"Well—"

"Keep it one-thousand."

"Well, I would've given him the chance to tell you first because that's only fair. If he didn't then I would've... So, to answer your question, yes. But I feel like he would've if it was a chance that she was possibly pregnant with his baby."

"You think he would've told me that?"

"Yea." Tiny responded.

"You think he would've told me that he was fucking my girl?" Jabari asked with an unpleasant scowl. "You can't possibly think that. Why you think I've been in the dark this long?"

"You're probably right, but I think a baby would've changed things."

"Man, I don't even wanna talk about this. It's still a pill that's hard to swallow." Jabari irritably said with a shake of the head.

"I'm sorry," Tiny apologized. "You probably think I'm very messy for even bringing this up."

"I don't know if being messy is the right terminology, but you definitely started some shit. A part of me wished you would've just left it alone, but then again I think I would've rather know. It ain't like I didn't have my suspicions."

"About Slick and her?"

"No, but about her and some other nigga."

"See, so you felt something."

Fallin' In Love With The Goat 3

"Yea, I did," Jabari admitted. "I never expected it was with my brother though."

"I know you didn't and when he told me I told him that he was wrong for that. However, he said he'd gotten caught up and he really was feeling her. All I know is that he used to give her money and look out for her when you were locked up. It was supposed to be just that, at least that's how he said it started out. Of course, a lonely night for her ended up being spent with him and then—"

"A'ight, I don't wanna hear no more. I get the picture." Jabari cut in.

"Look, I know we slept together back when we were teenagers. It was only once after a football game. I'll never forget, we were leading by 24-0."

"Yea, I remember. Those were the good ol' days."

"Yea, they were. I always liked you and even more after that night. But, I respected the fact that it wasn't going to be nothing more than what it was. I'm only bringing that up to say this. I don't want you to think that I told you about Cashmere just to try and get close with you. That's definitely not the reason. Whether you stay with her or not, I know we aren't gonna be together. I just thought it was the right thing to do."

Jabari nodded his head. "You're good, Tiny. It's better to know now than to have found out later. So, I appreciate your honesty."

"JAAAHH," Trudy called out, as she made her way to the front door. She walked out on the porch and then instantly wrapped her arms around Jabari's neck. He hugged her back, but didn't expect such a greeting, as tears started rolling down Trudy's face. Her small frame felt weak in his arms like she had been going through it.

By: Tiece

Trudy cried for a mere 3 minutes until she was able to breathe again. It was something about his presence that reminded her of Slick. Jabari felt choked up but held his composure. He comforted Trudy until she was finally able to let him go. She backed off from him and looked him up and down.

"I didn't realize I missed seeing you around this much. Just your company reminds me so much of my boy. The way you dress, the cologne you're wearing, that handsome smile—"

"Auntie, y'all come on in the house." Tiny cut in. "Jabari you want something to drink?"

"Sure, I'll have some water," Jabari said as he followed them into the house.

"Sit down, son. Sit down." Trudy insisted. "It's so good to see you." She said sitting down on the couch beside Jabari.

"It's really good to see you too. When I pulled up I didn't know if I'd be able to get out. It's still very hard for me without Slick being here."

"I know, I'm the same way." Trudy agreed. "It'll never be the same anymore. My world is now forever changed, and I don't know what to do about it."

"I know." Jabari said.

"Well, I've been wanting to talk with you. I know it's no easy way to say this, but I've been told that you are aware of what's going on."

Jabari frowned. "If you're talking about the baby then yes I know."

"So, you must also know that it's important for me to find out if the baby belongs to my son."

"I'm sure."

"He and I was always close, but of course within the past few years we had gotten super tight with each other. He made sure I was good and that my bills were paid. Even in his death he made sure that I'd be taken care of."

"Oh really?" Jabari pondered. He knew that Slick and his mom were cool, but what was she talking about?

"Taken care of? Did you find some money somewhere or something?"

"No, but he did leave a policy behind for me. I haven't even been able to go to his house. I don't believe I'll ever be able to go there. Packing his clothes, looking through his things is just not something I can do." Trudy explained. "The house is his though, so I know one day I'll have to sell it or rent it out, but I ain't trying to do nothing right now. I was hoping you'd go over and pack his things for me. You know, take some of the stuff to Goodwill and let them have it. I'm sure it's people that could use some of his stuff."

"Yea, I'm sure, but I don't think I can go there yet either. I'm just not in the right mind frame for that."

"I know," Trudy sadly said. "Have you heard anything? Do you know who could've done that to him?"

"No ma'am. We still don't know much about what happened. We aren't stopping until we find some answers though," he said, as Tiny returned with a glass of water. Instead of sitting down to listen in, she handed over the water and went outside to sit on the front porch.

"Well, Tiny did tell me what was going on and I would love to know if the baby that woman is carrying is my son's. I hate he did that to you, but I know my boy. His loyalty was with you. He loved you like a blood brother. I don't see how that betrayal even existed UNLESS that woman came on to him."

"It's a few speculations I've had about that too, but I can't let that get to me. It's over and done with and the only thing I can do is wait like everybody else."

"Well, do you think the baby is yours?"

"Honestly, I don't know what to think."

"I plan on reaching out to her soon. I would like to be there when the baby is born. I know it could be yours and I'm fine with that. You're like a son to me too, but I would like to get DNA results as soon as possible."

Jabari sat silently for a minute or two. He had to get his thoughts together. Could Cashmere actually be pregnant by Slick? It all seemed like one big nightmare that he was hoping he'd wake up from. Unfortunately, it looked like this was happening whether he liked it or not. *Damn, how could Cashmere be so fucking careless?* He pondered to himself.

"I know I'm jumping the gun, but if you talk to her can you please give her my number so she can call me. I would like to get to know the mother of my son's baby. If that's his baby."

Jabari stood to his feet, while sitting the glass of untouched water on the end table. Hearing those words made him cringe inside. He had yet to take all of that in. So, now to hear someone else being interested in a baby that was supposed to be his, had him deep in his feelings. "Yea, I'll do that." He nodded. "But, I'm gonna get out of here. If we hear anything about what happened you'll be the first to know."

"Thank you," Trudy said, as she grabbed Jabari and hugged him. It was clear that she was sick over losing Slick. He could feel her weary body trembling against his. It was definitely a surreal moment. Out the corner of his eye and over by the wall, he noticed a cane. He could remember seeing her back in the day walking on it. It was only a few times, because other times she was getting around just fine. He never asked questions but at that moment, he then realized that Slick really was her caretaker. He had looked out for Trudy for as long as he could remember. She struggled with an illness that he never knew of because Slick kept it under wraps for a long time. It wasn't until he was in prison that Slick wrote and told him that his mom struggled with a form of arthritis that prevented her from working. She had really good days and then really bad days.

Unfortunately, their high school graduation fell on one of those hard days and Trudy didn't attend. To them it looked like Trudy was selfish and out of touch with being there for her son. There were even times when Slick acted more like the adult and she was more of the child. He could even remember one night when they were around 16 years old, Slick wasn't feeling well, but that didn't stop Trudy from going out to party that night. The day after, she up and went to Miami Beach for 3 more days. Slick took care of himself. Now, he saw things for what it was. When Trudy felt good she lived it up, because it was only a matter of time before her bad days resurfaced. Nobody understood that more than Slick. He wasn't

By: Tiece

ashamed of her illness, but he protected her privacy. Not only that, but once he was old enough he promised that he would always take care of her, and that's what he did.

Once the loving embrace had run its course, Jabari stared in Trudy's eyes. "You alright?"

"No, but I will be."

"Well, you know I'm just a phone call away. I don't know if you have my number somewhere, but get it from Tiny—"

"I'll give it to you Auntie." Tiny chimed in, as she continued to rock in the chair.

"Don't hesitate to you use it." He insisted.

"I won't." Trudy told him. "Take care of yourself and be safe in these streets."

Jabari nodded his head with a half-smile on his face. "I will." He responded, and then looked at Tiny. "Be easy, alright."

"You too," Tiny said, and with that Jabari made his way out to the car and was out of sight within the blink of an eye.

Later that evening, Jabari sat on the front porch at his parent's 3-story, 5-bedroom house. It had always been the perfect place to relax at, and it held so many memories, 90% of them were good. Thoughts of him and Slick playing basketball, drinking, smoking, and clowning around crossed his mind, as a tear came to his eye. He missed his brother with all his heart. It hurt like hell every time he woke up knowing he wouldn't get a text or a call from him each day. He stood up and stretched his arms out, while taking in a deep breath. It wasn't the day to get lost in weary thoughts. It was Papers birthday, and everyone was inside enjoying themselves. As always, his mom had cooked a big dinner so they could celebrate. It was only family and close friends there, which made it an intimate affair and one with lots of drinks, music, loud laughs and good eating.

As he got himself together, he turned to rejoin the festivities, but stopped in his tracks as Justin walked out on the front porch to join him.

"They wildin' in there," Justin grinned while pointing back towards the inside of the house. "I had to come out for some fresh air and take a break from laughing."

Jabari shook his head with a slight grin. "Pops and Papers still in there going down memory lane?"

"Hell yea," Justin answered. "They just moved from the 1st level to the family room now." The bottom level was what they called the 1st level of the home or to some, the basement. It had its own section of the house, but was all in one large, long room with every perk and amenity one could think of. It even had 2 bathrooms.

"That means that the party is starting to wind down."

"Yea, you already know. It's just past ten o'clock and I'd say it's good timing. The party started at four sharp; so I'm sure they're about burnt out."

"They should be." Jabari laughed. "I know I am. Shit, I ain't even leaving. I'm staying the night here."

"I don't blame you. I might do the same thing, but that depends on how I'm feeling later when this chick gets off of work."

By: Tiece

"What chick?" Jabari pondered, while sitting back down in one of the chairs that lined the front porch. "What happened to you and Shyla? Y'all still ain't talking like that?"

"Nah, we don't really talk like that. I get it though, because her bitch ass ex is trying to stop her from moving on."

"What you mean by that?"

"Like when we first started kicking it, it was all good. But then the nigga showed up one day while I was over there. I didn't say nothing, I just left so they could talk. I ain't even trip on that because he is her kids' father, so you know how that is."

"Yea."

"Then I was over there another day, and he popped up again. He showed up with an attitude, trying to start with her and shit. The boys were there this time and I don't know if that triggered him, but he was deep in his feelings. Asking her not to have the boys around another man, all kinds of dumb shit. Like he ain't moved on and got a baby by another woman that's not even his wife." Justin added.

"Damn, we talking about Rich right?"

"Yea, the bitch that owns the Club's."

"Right, but he don't look like the type to begging for smoke."

"He ain't, that's why I backed off. I don't wanna have to lay this nigga out; especially in front of his boys." Justin told him.

"Damn, you might have to though. Sometimes, you gotta show a nigga what time it is, so he won't think it's sweet. Shit, I had to lay me a nigga out right on Tiana's front porch."

Justin laughed out loud. "Man, that shit made my stomach hurt when I heard about that. I laughed so hard."

"The shit was funny, but I know it scared the shit outta Tiana. She acted like she was gon' leave his ass there, but then she stayed just to make sure he was alright. Hell, I didn't care. I just needed for him to know when he see me or know that I'm over there, he better not show the fuck up."

Justin continued laughing. "I feel you, though Bruh. I can't even tell you if me and Shyla will get back on that level, but I'm being patient. She still checks in from time to time. I just don't be pushing the issue of even trying to see her like that. I be cooling. When she gets ready she'll let me know. Until then, I'm gon' keep my hittas on the team."

Jabari grinned. "Shit, I can't blame you."

Anika stepped out on the front porch. She had her purse and her keys in her hand. "Well, boys as always, it was great hanging out with y'all." She said.

"We're glad you always come through. For 7 years you've never let us down." Jabari said.

"Yea, we appreciate you. Mama really loves when you come around. Not only is your mom her childhood best friend, but you and Skylar were born around the same time which led to y'all becoming best friends."

"Call it destiny." Anika said. "We all were placed in each other's lives for a reason. Matter of fact, mama is still in there partying like it's 1999. I got a plane to catch in the morning. I gotta get back to the house and finish packing."

By: Tiece

"So, you're taking the job in New York?" Justin asked.

"Yea, I think it's time for me to spread my wings and see what else is out there for me. I'm 26 years old. By the time I'm 35 I wanna be settled down, married, and have babies in tow."

"Ain't nothing wrong with that." Jabari grinned. "Skylar would definitely wanna see you living your best life."

Anika nodded with a quaint smile on her face. "Yea, she would want that." She said, while giving the brothers a hug. She started to leave, but something more was on her mind. "You know there has been something that I've wanted to tell y'all about Skylar. I know it's been 7 years and I struggled with even telling y'all this, but Skylar wasn't pregnant by Mars."

Justin and Jabari's eyes stretched.

"Say what now?" Jabari pondered.

"That baby wasn't his and I believe she met up with him to tell him and that's why he killed her."

"So, you do think he killed her?" Justin asked.

"Yea, I do. I don't see who else would've done that."

"So, who was this guy that she was seeing?" Jabari asked.

"I don't know. She never told me that. She said she didn't want me to know but in due time she would tell. From some of the things we did talk about though, I know he was an older guy which is something that y'all probably wouldn't have approved of, especially your father. I also peeped that he was into racing. I think," she added. "You gotta know how Skylar was. She was super outgoing, but she knew how to carry a secret. She was very evasive when it came to him, but she did tell me that he made her happy. Come to think about it, she started seeing this guy months before she started seeing Mars. So, honestly I think Mars was just a cover-up. Unfortunately, he didn't know it."

"Wow," Justin uttered. "I've thought about this scenario, just not exactly how you explained it."

"Me too, and now the question is, who was this guy that Skylar was seeing?" Jabari pondered.

"I don't know, but if you find out who he is, I'm sure all the pieces will start to come together. I'm sure," Anika said, as she glanced down at her watch. "I ain't trying to rush off, but call me if you have any other questions. I've pondered over this for years, and I do feel it's past time for the truth to come to the light."

"I agree." Justin said. "Take care of yourself."

"And, safe travels. We're also here if ever need us." Jabari added.

"I know," Anika said, with a smile. "See ya later alligators," she teased.

Jabari and Justin looked over at each other, just as Bruno and Melissa exited the house.

"Y'all leaving too?" Jabari asked, as he cleared his throat.

"Yea, I think it's time we got out of here. We've had so much fun." Bruno assured them with a light chuckle. "It's always good to be around family."

"We're glad y'all came." Jabari said, as he reached out to shake Bruno's hand. "Y'all good? Y'all don't need a ride?"

Bruno shook his head. "Oh, nah. We called Lyft this year. People don't ever leave a McCoy party and not be lit."

By: Tiece

"He's right," Melissa said, with a big smile on her face. "We're feeling good and tonight just might be the night."

"Melissa," Bruno eased in.

Justin frowned. "The night for what?"

"The night for us to try to conceive again." Melissa told him.

"From the way y'all look I believe it'll happen tonight." Justin teased.

"Yea, for some reason I can feel it." Melissa beamed.

"Well, congrats," Jabari said, as if her saying that confirmed the news.

"Yea, well—" Bruno attempted to say but was cut off by Melissa.

"On top of that, we may be moving in a few months if everything works out."

Jabari frowned. "Oh yea?"

"We're looking for property now." Melissa chimed in.

"Big guy you didn't tell us that y'all may be moving."

"That's because we don't know that for sure yet." Bruno reluctantly answered, while clearing his throat and then checking the time on his watch. "Melissa wants a fresh start; especially with us looking forward to having a baby. She's had all the surgeries she needed in removing the cysts."

"Surgeries that I'm glad are behind me now."

"That's right and since then we've been talking about a fresh start. Of course, I was going to tell y'all about it. We just haven't made for sure plans yet."

Fallin' In Love With The Goat 3

"I see," Jabari uttered.

"Aaaand, here's our Lyft driver. You ready babe?"

"Yea, see y'all later." Melissa waved, as she quickly headed down the steps.

"Until next time," Bruno said, giving the brother's dap. "I'll see y'all next week."

"A'ight." Jabari and Justin said. The minute the lovebirds were out of sight the brother's looked at each other. Something didn't sit right, and it wasn't just with one of them. They both felt it.

Chapter Eight

Jabari walked into the kitchen where Justin was already sitting at the table drinking a mug of caramel cappuccino, and their mom was standing behind the stove preparing breakfast. "I thought I smelled breakfast cooking."

"You know how mom is." Justin uttered.

"Well, I'm glad y'all stayed the night. That doesn't happen too often since y'all are grown." Mrs. McCoy said, while stirring the grits.

"We had a lot of leftovers we could've ate on that." Jabari told her.

"Nonsense, you know I don't mind cooking. Want some coffee or cappuccino?"

"No ma'am," Jabari answered while going towards the refrigerator. "I just want some O.J."

"The party last night was lit." Justin chimed in, while sipping from his mug. "It felt so good to see everybody in such a good space. Everybody that was here had a good time."

"Yea, it was really nice." Mrs. McCoy inserted. "I did enjoy myself. As always it was good to see Anika. She's so busy these days."

"Yea, she told us she's taking a job in New York. She's thinks it's time for her to spread her wings." Justin revealed.

"That's good for her. She should spread her wings and enjoy her life. I'm proud of her." Mrs. McCoy said.

"We all are," Biggs said as he entered the kitchen. "It smells good in here Darling. We could've ate leftovers, ya know?"

"Same thing I said Pops."

"Nobody's eating leftovers unless you decide to eat it after breakfast." Mrs. McCoy said.

"Speaking of moving," Jabari said while sitting down next to Justin at the table. "Melissa and Bruno was feeling real good last night. Melissa even mentioned something about them moving."

"Somewhere here?" Mrs. McCoy asked.

"Nah, I didn't get the feeling that it would be here. Bruno said something about them making a fresh start somewhere else." Justin told them.

"That's strange." Biggs uttered.

"It's a lot of things that's pretty strange when it comes to Bruno." Jabari agreed. "I was told that Bruno was moving weight for Slick."

Biggs and Justin frowned.

"And, you're just telling us that?" Biggs pondered, as Mrs. McCoy handed him a cup of coffee.

"I've just been sitting back and watching how he moves. Honestly, he's moving funny, but we've not looked at him in that manner, so it's gone over our heads." Jabari explained.

"He's definitely moving funny if he was working with Slick. We all know how Bruno is big on not wanting to have anything to do with drugs. He's strictly about cars and racing. That's how he has always made his money." Justin explained.

By: Tiece

"Well, what are you suggesting?" Biggs asked.

"I don't know, but something is off with him." Jabari responded.

"You don't think he's hiding more than just working for Slick do you? Plus, wouldn't Slick have told you if Bruno was working with him?" Mrs. McCoy asked.

"Slick was like a brother to me, but he didn't tell me everything that was going on with him." He answered.

"Well, you're right about that." Mrs. McCoy agreed, as she thought about Slick possibly being Cashmere's baby daddy.

"I don't know, y'all. Slick was on to something and he told me the night he died. The person that he's been talking about was said to be close in our circle. I don't know too many people that's really close in our circle."

"But is he that close? Meaning as close as Bruno has been in our family. Bruno is family and I don't know, but he didn't have a reason to kill Slick."

"But if Slick was on to him—"

"Then you never know," Justin agreed with his brother, while also completing his sentence.

Biggs sat down at the table while sipping on his coffee. "Well, I know Papers is sleeping in this morning, but I definitely need to bring this to his attention. I don't want to think that Bruno is involved in Slick's death, but I have to check everybody out."

"Please do, because not only were they talking about moving, but they were talking about her finally conceiving."

"What?" Mrs. McCoy cut in. "She ain't had no baby in all this time, I doubt it will happen now."

"Well, he said that she's had all the surgeries she needed to have and so their chances were pretty high." Justin informed them.

"Yea, that is what he said," Jabari confirmed.

"I'll have to see it to believe it." Mrs. McCoy uttered.

"Well, I went to visit Ms. Trudy yesterday morning."

"How did that go? How is she doing?" Mrs. McCoy asked.

"She's holding up pretty good, I guess. I know financially she seems to be straight. She mentioned that Slick had left her a policy."

Biggs nodded his head. "Yea, he did that a few years back. I advised him, since he had come to me for help in getting a policy drawn up. If I'm not mistaken, Trudy should have gotten about a half-million dollars from that policy, unless Slick changed it."

"Nah, I believe it's about that much." Jabari said. "She's getting work done on her house, new roof and all. The place was immaculate with new furniture. I could smell the new, new inside the house. Plus, she getting a space added on the back for Tiny since she's moving in."

"Well, that's good. Tiny can now take care of her. I guess they'll be taking care of each other." Mrs. McCoy said. "So, did you just show up there?"

"No ma'am. Tiny messaged me and told me Ms. Trudy wanted to see me." He said.

By: Tiece

"What was that about?" Justin pondered. "I mean, I know she's still grieving and all."

"Yea, she is. She hugged me so hard I could literally feel her body shaking in my arms. She almost made me cry because she couldn't stop crying."

"Awww, that's the saddest thing ever. We know that feeling all too well." Mrs. McCoy said, as she sat Biggs breakfast plate in front of him, followed by the brothers.

"I know right." Justin uttered.

"So, but why did Trudy want to see you?" Mrs. McCoy asked.

"She basically wanted to talk with me about Cashmere's baby. She said that she wants to be a part of the baby's life if it's Slick's. Which also means that when the baby is born she's also wants to get a DNA test done."

"Well, you can't blame her." Biggs said. "She lost a son. This could be his legacy that lives on and I can understand her wanting to be a part of that."

Jabari hunched his shoulders. "I get it." He agreed.

"I just hate that y'all have to go through this. It's such a sad thing. I can only imagine what Cashmere is going through. This has to be hard on her too." Mrs. McCoy said, while chewing her bacon. "Did you tell Cashmere that you spoke with Trudy yet?"

"Not yet," he responded.

"Y'all still aren't really talking?" Biggs questioned, and then sipped from his coffee.

"Not really," Jabari answered. "I just wanna find out as quickly as possible if this baby is mine. If it's not, I'm completely done with her. If it is, I'll do my part as the father but I still don't see myself being with her."

Mrs. McCoy shook her head. "Nobody wins in this situation, especially the baby."

"You're right," Biggs said. "Well, on another note, Tonio races Stunner next weekend."

"He gon' get his butt beat again." Justin laughed.

"But he knows how to bring a crowd. That nigga be seriously stunnin'. He got the right name. I enjoyed whooping his butt." Jabari laughed.

"I think him racing Tonio is more his speed. He's good but he's not ready for the big dogs." Biggs said.

"I agree." Jabari concurred. "Bruno is set to race Roy too right?"

"Yep, that should be a good race too. I'm surprised neither wants to get ready for a rematch with you, but then again I'm not. They usually try to pick on somebody they feel they can beat before they challenge the person that beats them."

"True," Justin chimed in.

"They ain't ready anyway. Getting embarrassed 2 times in a row ain't no joke. Just ask me." Jabari said.

"So, when do you plan on asking Ace for a rematch. I know you ready to redeem yourself."

"Honestly, I don't know. I know the challenge is coming soon. I don't know if I'll be the one to call him out or if he'll be the one that calls me out. I guess we'll see."

"He's probably waiting on you, while you're sitting over here waiting on him." Justin said.

"Technically, I'm not waiting on him. I've won 2 races already since I've been home. I'm really just trying to stay focused. I wanted to rebuild my brand a little before jumping back on the strip with him, anyway. You know, let my fans know that I was back. So, when I whoop his tail they'll know it's real."

Justin grinned. "I feel you."

"Well, from this point on, we need to keep our friends close and our enemies closer. We'll be doing test runs this week. Talk to Bruno not about Slick, but see what he got going on. For the most part, get in his head. We need to get him to slip and if he's really hiding something he will. My thing is that I can't wrap my brain around knowing that he was a part of Slick's death. That's just hard for me to believe. But, if y'all feel that something is off then it probably is. I've just been looking in the wrong direction because of the trust I put in him. But, I can't keep looking away from something that could be staring me right in the face."

"I agree Pops," Justin said. "So, from this point on we just need to talk to him more. We can even act like we've heard something else on the streets, something that could make him break. Whatever it is we have to apply pressure. As much pressure as we can but without him really knowing that we're testing him." He said, and then looked over at Jabari. "Whatever happened to the guy that said he was Mar's cousin? Does he still plan on talking to you? I've been curious since he showed up."

"Yea, me too, but Buddy won't holla at me. I don't know what he's got going on. I hit him up a few times with no response or text back. I just figure if he really got something to say he'll hit me up."

"He's not even here anymore. I've already looked into it." Biggs said, "But I got a feeling he'll be returning for some reason. Whatever the hell is going on it's deep and the more we look into it the deeper it's gonna get. I can't say if Slick's death and Skylar's are related, but I do believe finding out about one will somehow lead us to the other. I just hate to think Bruno could be involved." Biggs said with a shake of the head. The last thing he wanted was beef with someone that was like a family member to him. It was even hard to point the finger his way. It actually hurt him to his heart just to think that somebody that close to them could be so deceptive.

"You okay Pops?" Jabari pondered.

"Yea, I'm good. This is just a hard pill to swallow."

"Well, while we're on the subject of deceit. It seems that baby sister was hiding something." Jabari slid in.

Mrs. McCoy frowned. "Hiding what?"

"She was indeed seeing another man. I know we've talked about it before, but Anika confirmed it. She didn't know who this guy was, but she did know that Skylar was keeping him a secret—"

"And, that she was using Mars as a cover-up. Not to mention, that guy was Skylar's baby's daddy." Justin added.

"Possibly," Jabari said. "I really don't know what to believe anymore."

By: Tiece

"And, that's why we're having forensics ran for DNA matches." Biggs said. "They did say it could be months before results come back."

"If anything comes back." Mrs. McCoy added. "There is a chance that nothing comes to light."

"It is, so if nothing comes back then we move on to plan B." Biggs said, just as Jabari's cell phone chirped of an incoming text message.

He looked down at the display screen of his phone. "I think y'all talked her up." He said opening the message to read it.

"Who?" Mrs. McCoy pondered.

"Cash," he responded, while reading the text.

I know it's last minute, my apologies for that, but I just wanted to invite you to the baby's gender reveal today at 4 o'clock. It's going to be at Shyla's house. I really hope you come. Attached is the invitation. CASHMERE

"You good Bruh?" Justin pondered.

"Yea, she's inviting me to the baby's gender reveal." He responded.

"Well, that's sweet. I'm sure she's having a really nice one. What's the theme?" Mrs. McCoy asked.

Jabari pulled up the invite and handed his phone across the table to his mom. "Looks like it's either a Prince or a Princess."

Mrs. McCoy took the phone to look at the invite. She smiled. "I like this, it's so cute. I've seen some nice ones on social media, as well."

"Mama, you need to stay off Instagram." Justin teased.

"All she do is be liking everybody pictures." Jabari grinned.

"Just because I'm your mother doesn't mean that I can't have a social media account." She teased back.

"She be trying to tell me about people that she went to school with. They're always inviting her somewhere that she doesn't go, and on top of that she knows everybody's business." Biggs grinned.

"That's because everybody puts their business on there." Justin added.

"Well, are you going to go?" Mrs. McCoy asked Jabari.

He shrugged his shoulders. "Honestly, I don't know."

"Do what you feel is right son, follow your heart." Biggs told him. "One thing I do know is that you'll be a great dad if that baby is yours. I can understand you not wanting to get too caught up right now, just because of the circumstances. Just don't be like your brother."

Jabari grinned with a shake of the head. "He is trying though Pops."

"But he knew them children was his. Hell, when your mama showed me their pictures on Intragram—"

Jabari and Justin laughed out loud. "Say what now Pops?" Justin joked. "It's InSTagram."

"Leave your father alone." Mrs. McCoy laughed.

"Anyway, whatever the hell it is. But when your mother showed me them babies, I knew they were McCoy's."

"Mama how long you knew?" Jabari asked.

By: Tiece

"I found out about his daughter right before he had the DNA tests done and the same thing with his son. Once he came to me talking about Lauren was tripping after hearing something in the streets, I already knew what time it was. I insisted he got those tests done for both babies. Of course, they were done about a year a part." She added.

"You don't wanna be like him son. Get the DNA test done the first chance you get. That way you don't miss out on no time with your baby."

"That's the plan." Jabari said.

"From day one with each of you I was there. Even when your mom kicked me out I was still there for y'all. I made sure to make time, even when I felt I didn't have any. I would pick y'all up and take y'all to the shop with me and just let y'all run wild. That's how y'all got into cars at such young ages, sitting around watching me."

"Yea, and you always made sure we were at the dragstrip to watch you race. Cain was happy when his son there. I think that really made his night." Justin said.

"It should've because it made mine to see him there." Biggs smiled. "One thing about it, I've always loved my children and I'll do anything in the world for y'all."

"We know." Jabari said with a smile.

"Son, I think you should let Cashmere know what Trudy said, and at least give her the opportunity to invite her, whether you go or not." Mrs. McCoy said, while handing Jabari his phone back.

Jabari nodded his head. "You're right Ma and I will. Matter of fact, I'll let her know now."

Chapter Nine

Shyla stood inside of the large white tent admiring the décor of Cashmere's gender reveal. She didn't need it to be too much, but she definitely wanted it to be a special moment for her bestie. Cashmere had been going through a lot emotionally, and Shyla felt her pain. If she could make things a little better for her then that's what she was going to do. She smiled at the oversized royal chair specifically for the mom-to-be. It was decorated on one side with blue ribbons that had the word Prince on them and decorated on the other side with pink ribbons that had the word Princess on them. She also had a King's chair, not too far on stand-by just in case Jabari showed up. What she wasn't going to do was have it next to Cashmere's throne with nobody sitting in it.

The tent was filled with floating pink and blue balloons. The pink ones had a baby boy wearing a crown and the word Prince written all over it. The blue ones were opposite with a baby girl wearing a crown and the word Princess written all over them. It was like the blue offset the pink and vice versa.

Over on one side of the tent was a Prince or Princess backdrop for the guests to take pictures. There was a beautiful dessert table sitting closest to the royal chair. On top of the table was a large cake with blue and pink icing swirled all over it, each color standing out like a 3D affect. The side base of the cake had Princess written on one-side, and Prince on the other. The top centerpieces were two chubby brown skin babies, both wearing crowns, one a boy and the other a girl. The baby boy had on a blue diaper and the baby girl had on a pink diaper. On top of another table was the buffet of good food. There were 2 large pitchers one filled with pink hunch punch and the other filled with blue hunch punch. The punch was for the grown and sexy, since no kids were allowed. Cashmere would drink separately from her guests and anybody else that wasn't a drinker. Last but not least, on the other table there were pink and blue gift bags filled with Thank You cards, small bottles of liquor, and a few other goodies to show Cashmere's appreciation for them coming.

To top of the party was a DJ booth over in the corner. The object was to invite a few of their cousins, moms, aunties and close friends there. They were going to party, eat good food and drink top shelf liquor while playing games, dancing, and laughing the evening away. It was the perfect event to celebrate such a joyous occasion. She couldn't wait until Cashmere sees what the baby was going to be. The excitement alone was eating her up.

As she walked over to taste one of the meatballs, she could see someone entering the tent out of the corner of her eye. Quickly, she turned to see who it was.

"What the hell are you doing here Rich? I've asked you to call me before showing up to my house."

"I keep telling you that I don't have to call first with my boys being here."

Shyla scowled with a shake of the head. "Your boys aren't here, so you're definitely not welcomed. Matter of fact, whether they're here are not, you're not welcome to just show up at my house anymore."

Fallin' In Love With The Goat 3

"And, who's going to stop me?" Rich pondered, as he picked up a meatball with a toothpick and ate it. "This is good stuff." He smirked.

"Quit eating the food. It's not for you." Shyla spat. "And, to answer your question, the cops are gonna stop you."

"The cops? You wouldn't do that to me."

"Oh yea? Try me Rich. I'm sick of yo' ass and the next time you show up unannounced, the police will be called. I'm done playing these games with you. Matter of fact, I know my mama didn't let you in and didn't tell me—" she said while wanting to head in the house and check her mama.

"Man, calm down. I came through the fence. Your mama don't even know I'm out here." He quickly explained.

"Well, you need to be finding yo' pale ass back through the fence and out my face." Shyla said, as Rich pulled back his shirt to show off his gun. "What the fuck!?" Shyla shouted. "Are you fucking threatening me? You know you've taken this to a whole new level, right?"

"I'm not threatening you, so chill out. But, let me tell you something or better yet you can take this as a warning. I'm not letting you shut me out of my boys life."

"Like seriously? You can't be serious right now."

"Oh, I'm very serious." Rich told her.

Shyla looked him over. He didn't look like he could hurt a fly, but then again, looks could be deceiving. After all, he had already played her so good that she had no clue about the other woman or the baby he'd had outside of her boys. She didn't know if he was really trying to intimidate her or not. The only problem was that he had never showed that side before, let alone flashing a gun her way.

"Let me explain something to you because I don't believe you get it either. I've never shut you out of River and Ryder's life and I never will. However, if you ever showcase a gun in my presence again, I will do what I have to do to protect me and the boys. Do you understand?"

Rich shrugged a little while eating another meatball.

"And, you must know that I'm moving the fuck on with someone other than you."

"I know you ain't talking about that McCoy boy. He can't give you what you want."

Shyla rolled her eyes. "How do you know? He's already given me way more than you could ever give," she said, while glancing down at Rich's dick print. "That's right, it's really nothing there. If it wasn't for your pussy eating skills you would've been thrown to the wolves."

Rich grinned. "You weren't complaining when I was beatin' that pussy up and wearing yo' ass out."

"Maybe not, but you're not the only one that can put on, make up shit, and tell lies." She told him. "Just so you know, out of respect for our situation right now, when I have company I'll make sure the boys are at mama's house. But don't think that'll go on forever."

"Okay fine, and I'm taking them wherever I want them to go too."

"I would appreciate if you didn't. You didn't want to take them around your wife, so don't think you're taking them around your other bitch."

"I'll do what I want to do, since it's clear you keep wanting to play with me."

"Rich, just leave. If I hear my kids are around that bitch you won't see them again."

"You must be crazy if you think I'll sit back and ever allow that to happen. Woman, you got my clubs in your name and you knew what time it was when we first started fucking. So, why should it matter who else I'm with? Either way you knew I was with somebody else."

Rich quickly grabbed the side of his face, with an intimidated frown and a bit of fear in his glossy eyes. Shyla had slapped the shit out of him so hard spit flew out his mouth. He was still standing there looking like he didn't know what had just happened.

"What happened?" he asked like he was bugging or something.

"If you don't leave my house right now, I will gut you from yo' asshole to yo' muthafuckin' ear tips!" Shyla demanded, while grabbing the knife off the table that sat by the pink and blue icing covered cake.

Net entered the tent. "What's going on?!" she asked with a concerned, yet ready for whatever expression.

"Nothing," Rich quickly answered. "I was just leaving."

"Yea, he was just leaving, and he won't be coming back until he get his shit and his attitude together." Shyla said while shaking the knife in Rich's face.

"Alright Shyla. I got you!" Rich said while exiting the tent.

Net walked over to her daughter. "You okay?"

"Yea," Shyla said, as Net eased the knife out of her hands.

"If this relationship has turned to this it's definitely time for you to start looking out for yourself and to take out a damn restraining order on his ass if he keeps it up."

"I'm trying to spare this nigga because of Ryder and River, but he's making it extremely hard to be cordial with his ass."

I see. I thought he was about to get a slicing from the rooter to the tooter." Net laughed but was definitely serious.

"He was, while he out here thinking he can talk to me any kind of way."

"I told you his ass wasn't shit."

"I knoooow Ma, dang. You ain't gotta keep telling me either. You starting to sound like a broken record."

"Well, clean it off and maybe it'll stop scratching." Net shot her daughter's way. "I never cared for his ass."

"I knoooow." Shyla said, as she poured her a cup of blue hunch punch. "I need this." She said, while gulping the whole cup down in one swallow it seemed.

"Damn, slow down before your ass get choked."

"I'm good," Shyla said, as Spinderella, the DJ entered the tent. Quickly, she put on a fake smile and then looked over at her mother. "A'ight, it's about time to start mingling. We'll talk about this later."

"Okaaaay," Net sang with a shake of the head.

Fallin' In Love With The Goat 3

After speaking with Spinderella and helping her get set up, her cell phone rang. She pulled it out the pocket of her floral blue, pink and white bell-bottom pants. She looked at the display screen to see that it was Cashmere calling. She walked off to the side of the tent to talk with her privately.

"Where you at?"

"Dang, well hey to you too."

"I talked to you this morning, so technically we already spoke. Now, where you at? Your guests have already started coming in. Everybody that has walked in has brought a pack of pampers. Some even brought big boxes too. Auntie just showed up with a big box of pampers and a gift bag full of clothes."

"Auntie as in Jeanie? Like my mama?"

"Yep," Shyla answered. "She is really excited about being a grandma. She said she had some more stuff in the car. I told her just keep all that until the baby shower. We only asked for pampers during the reveal."

"Oh well—"

"Where are you?"

"I'm in your room?"

"In who room?" Shyla asked with a frown on her face.

"In your house inside your room," she answered.

"Why the hell are you in the house? You should be out here mingling with your guests."

"I know, but I'm nervous. I kinda wanna call this thing off." She said in a nervous, saddened tone.

By: Tiece

"Girl, you can't call off something that has already started. Just breath in and out, I'm bout to come in there." Shyla said, as she looked around at the guest. They seemed to be enjoying each other, eating, laughing and drinking. Nobody was looking for Cashmere yet, so she quickly slipped out to go check on her cousin.

"Hey, come here." Shyla said, upon walking in the bedroom to Cashmere shedding tears. "What's wrong? You okay?"

"No," Cashmere sniffed.

"Why, what's wrong Bestie?"

"Well, Jabari called me—"

"Is he coming or not?" Shyla butted in, almost with an attitude.

"That's not why he was calling." Cashmere said.

"Well, what did he want that's got you so upset?"

"He said that he talked to Slick's mother yesterday morning."

"Oh," Shyla mumbled, now completely out of words to say.

"He said that Tiny told her everything."

"Go fucking figure," Shyla uttered.

"Well, anyway she asked him about my baby and wants to have the tests done, so she'll know if he's Slicks."

"Damn, this really is happening."

"Yes, it is. Like I've not wanted to think about it because my baby comes first. If I have to be mommy and daddy that's what it'll be. But, now he's calling on the day of my gender reveal to tell me this shit. He said that with me having this gender reveal his mama may want to come if she knows about it."

"Yea, but she ain't gotta be nowhere in this picture right now. Not until we know for sure if she's the baby's grandma."

Cashmere sniffed while wiping her eyes. "That's what I was thinking, but what if I'm being selfish? Her son is gone, and this could be the highlight of her world just to be here, but then on the other hand, I don't wanna get her too involved and then the baby ends up being Jabari's. That would surely break her heart."

"I know it would, that's why I say don't tell her. Just let her know after you've had him. I mean, I can even call her for you when you go into labor. She can come to the hospital like everybody else."

"That sounds so cold though. The woman just lost her only son. That's gotta be devastating for her because for me, I'm stuck because I know part of what she's feeling. So, I know she's heartbroken to the core."

"Now, get yourself together. You have guests outside waiting for you and the DJ has it crunk out there." Shyla coached.

Cashmere nodded her head, as she walked in the master bathroom. "Okay, give me a few minutes. I'll be out there. I just gotta check my make-up."

"You're going to love it when you see it. I didn't think it was going to turn out to be so beautiful."

"Ooooh, I'm so excited. Go entertain until I make it out there. Matter of fact, can you record and send me the video of how it looks. I'm going to send it to Jabari."

"And, there you go still thinking about Jabari."

"I can't help it. Can you please do that for me?"

"Yes, now get it together and make it quick." Shyla insisted.

"Okaaaay, I'm coming."

Jabari had been parked and sitting in his car for the past 30 minutes. All types of thoughts were going through his head. It was hard to figure things out, if only his problems could be solved overnight and the next morning he could wake up refreshed, thinking clearly, and moving forward. However, it wasn't that easy. Had it not been for a baby involved he would be able to move on. He slightly shook his head, with irritable thoughts continuing to flow, just as his phone alerted him of a text message. He glanced down at his phone and then picked it up off the arm rest to check it out.

Wassup Jabari. This is Leo. I know I was supposed to meet up with you but I returned home due to some unexpected issues. Whenever I return I'll reach back out. LEO

Jabari frowned. "What's up with this nigga?" he pondered to himself and then messaged back.

Yo, I really wanna need to know what you had to tell me. I know it had to be something important for you to come to my sister's event and unannounced at that. We're at a very critical moment here in trying to find out what really happened surrounding my sister's death. It could even be something that's forthcoming in clearing your cousin. He might decide to come out of hiding if that's the case. On top of that, it's connected to Slick's untimely death, as well. So, I hope you can see how important this is for me. JAH

Fallin' In Love With The Goat 3

In no time, Leo was messaging back.

I heard about Slick's death. I'm sorry about that, but everything that I spoke to him about is now clouding my judgement. What I thought I knew, I realized I didn't. The information I have is now no longer something I want to share. LEO

A perplexed expression covered Jabari's face. "What information?" he questioned to himself. "What fucking information?!"

Aye man, just let me determine that. The info you have could possibly help us with so many unanswered questions. JAH

Jabari sat waiting for a response. A few minutes passed and still no response.

You still there? JAH

About 15 minutes later, still no response.

"Fuck, he trippin'." Jabari uttered, just as his cell phone alerted him of an incoming text message. "Bout time." He quickly opened the message, but it wasn't who he was expecting.

Hey Jah, this is Shyla. Cashmere wasn't sure if you were coming to the gender reveal, but we're a little past an hour in and Cashmere is getting anxious. She's ready to see what the baby is. So, even though I recorded earlier, I'm recording this moment as well. I prefer to send you this one instead. I'll also send over a few pictures for keepsake. You can just let me know if you want them. SHYLA

Attached to the text was a video. Jabari began to play the video, as he looked at how extravagant the event was. He never thought it was so much thought and decor that went into a gender reveal. To him, that was unnecessary money spent that could've gone into a trust account for the baby. Not only that, but then a baby shower would follow which was the craziest thing ever.

Nevertheless, it was a beautiful moment causing his heart to flutter with excitement of finding out what the baby was.

"Say cheeeese, Bestie!" Shyla said, as she walked over recording with her phone. "Wave to your viewers!"

"Heyy," Cashmere waved in the camera with a big bright smile on her face. She stood up from her throne, long blonde hair with the dark roots slayed with big curls, make-up on fleek, and dressed in a baby blue and white fitted, Moschino T-shirt dress that stopped a few inches above her knees. She had on a pair of baby blue and white Moschino sneakers to match. She was definitely dressed according to what she wished was baking in her oven. While laughing with her friends and family, everyone made their way outside the tent.

"You couldn't have done this on a more beautiful day." Jeanie chimed with an elated tone.

"Yes, it's the perfect look of fall starting to set in." Net agreed.

"Oh my God, not a piñata?" Cashmere grinned. She was excited to see the big piñata covered in babies with either blue or pink diapers on.

Shyla gave her a wooden bat.

"I didn't see this here before entering the tent." Cashmere said.

"I know. It was meant to be a surprise. Ma, didn't hang it until we were all inside the tent."

"Wow, I love this Bestie."

"I knew you would. So, swing hard as you can." Shyla told her.

"I'll try." Cashmere joked, as everyone stood around, still dancing to the music that was playing in the background, with a bit of chatter and excitement. Cashmere stood back with the bat in her hands.

"Hold up," Shyla quickly cut in. "Tell the viewers what you wanna have."

Cashmere smiled as she looked at herself in the video camera. "Well, as you can see from my attire, I would love to have a boy!" she happily shrieked. "It's going to be a boy, watch what I tell you!"

Shyla laughed out loud, "Well, let's find out."

Cashmere stood back in position again and swung at the piñata. It didn't seem to budge. "Damn, this thing is hard." she let out. "Bestie what you got in this thing?"

"The answer to your prayers." she teased.

"Let me help you," Jeanie joyfully jumped in.

"I don't mind if you do," Cashmere responded, as she handed Jeanie the bat.

"Stand back y'all." Jeanie screamed out, and with that she hit the piñata. Again, it didn't budge. Everybody burst out laughing.

"Auntie, you need help too." Shyla chuckled, while giving Net a wooden bat too. "Help her Ma."

By: Tiece

"Okay, let's break inside this animal, Jeanie. My niece tryna see what she's having."

Jeanie and Net swung at the pinata. Swing after swing, and finally it cracked.

"Bout time," Cashmere let out, as she continued laughing at how funny it was seeing her mom and auntie swinging the bats like little kids while they joked around. They had everybody laughing with their crazy banter. Finally, Jeanie swung the bat with all her might and suddenly, pink wrapped candy and confetti came falling from it. Everybody screamed out in excitement, including Cashmere. She was shocked because she had surely predicted it was a boy, but either way she was still elated. Happy tears started to fall from her eyes. "Wow, I'm so excited," she let out. "I thought it was a boy. I just knew it was freaking a boy!" she joked with laughter. "But it's okay, I'll love my mini-me all the same."

Shyla smiled, as the joyful tears began to fill her eyes. "I'm so happy for you Bestie. Now, you can stop wearing all that blue."

Cashmere laughed. "Well too bad, because she's going to wear blue sometimes too." She teased, as Shyla looked in the camera.

"It's a GIRL!"

Jabari smiled, while wiping the teardrop that he stubbornly tried to restrain. Watching that video was the most touching thing he'd experienced in a long time. Cashmere was beautiful. She looked happy which gave him a sense of relief for some reason. Even though he'd been acting an ass, it wasn't meant for the baby or her well-being.

Fallin' In Love With The Goat 3

He knew in his mind that he had to do better. As he sat in his car, looking around the nice, suburban neighborhood, thoughts of wanting to get out crossed his mind. After all, he'd been parked there for a while now. However, as he reached for the door latch to open his car door a familiar face caught his attention, as the lady walked towards the house. It was Trudy walking up the driveway with a box of pampers.

Jabari approvingly nodded his head with a slight smile on his face. Cashmere didn't seem too eager in her messages to invite Trudy over, but maybe she was trying to be a better person. Instead of negatively feeling some type of way about it, a satisfied expression appeared on his face. "Good girl Cash. Good girl." He whispered, while starting his engine and swiftly leaving the neighborhood.

By: Tiece

Chapter Ten

Cain stood at the front door, knocking and ringing the doorbell simultaneously. The door flew open, as Hazel appeared in the doorway with her hand on her hip. Clearly, she wasn't too pleased about his unannounced visit.

"Why are you here ringing my bell and knocking on my door like you're crazy? What's your problem Cain?"

Cain walked straight in her house passing her. Hazel smacked her lips while closing the door back shut.

"You gonna answer me or nah?" she asked with an agitated expression.

"So, what you mean sending me that text message you're about to get married?"

"Exactly what I said. Me telling you that shouldn't have prompted you to bring your ass over here."

"The hell you preach." Cain responded with angry eyes. "I didn't even know you were seeing somebody. You don't be posting the nigga on your pages, so he gotta be a nobody."

Hazel smirked with a shake of the head. "Are you serious? Just because I don't post pictures of him doesn't mean I'm not seeing someone. Only small-minded people would think like that."

"Oh, so I'm small-minded now?"

"Apparently," she answered. "Why should it bother you that I'm getting married, anyway? Don't you have a woman?" she asked but quickly answered for him. "You do, and she's a pretty cool female."

"That's why you wanted to get to know her."

"What?" Hazel asked with a slick roll of the eyes.

"Because you knew you had my baby hanging around another nigga and if I found out I'd be mad." He griped.

"Mad?" Hazel frowned. "First, off we decided when I got pregnant that we were going to cordially go our separate ways, because you were in a relationship and I wasn't with it no more. You said you'd do right by Navaeh and come see her when time was available. Yes, you do send money all the time, but you don't come see her like that. I wanted to be fair in letting you be a part of her life, so there weren't any excuses when you did find out I had moved on. That's why I met up with your woman."

"First off, let's take this shit back a little since it seems that you suddenly have amnesia. We were together for 4 years."

"And the whole 4 years you were with someone else."

"That's not the point." Cain cut in. "Let me finish."

Hazel sat down on the couch and crossed her arms. "Go ahead, finish." She irritably uttered.

"I know you had given me ultimatums over the years and I wouldn't half do right, but I loved you. You knew that. Hell, I was with you more than I was with my woman."

"But you wouldn't leave her."

"That was a little more complicated and you knew it."

By: Tiece

"Doesn't matter."

"Yes, it does, because the last time you gave me an ultimatum, I chose you, yet you walked away." He explained.

"Yea, but I had my reasons. Plus, I didn't think you'd fully commit to being with me." Hazel responded.

"I really was going to be with you. I had made up my mind. I met at the spot you wanted us to meet at and sat there for hours, but you never showed up. I called your phone, texted, everything, still you didn't come."

"Why must we keep walking down such a disheartening memory lane?"

"Because I really wanted to be with you. Then you disappeared for months and when you showed back up you were only a couple months shy of having our baby. You even tried to deny that she was mine, but you knew I'd find out the truth sooner or later."

"Yet, you didn't claim her to the world until you had a DNA test done."

"I had to have that because my mom asked me to." He said.

"Yea, right. She looks just like a McCoy. I believe your woman wanted you to, but that's neither here nor there. Hell, as long as that money was still coming in, I didn't care what you asked for." She said.

"Oh, so it's all about the money now?"

Hazel frowned. "Don't go there. I have my own money. I take care of me and can very well take care of Navaeh. I'm not a housewife like your woman."

Fallin' In Love With The Goat 3

"Why you keep bringing her up?"

"To make a point." Hazel responded.

"Don't play with me." He cut in.

"Cain, the point I'm proving here is that it's been well over 3 years since we've been in that space of loving each other. Hell, our daughter is soon to turn 3."

"But I still love you."

Hazel shook her head. "That's something you have to deal with but I've moved on. I'm not wasting anymore time in a relationship with somebody and I not wholeheartedly know where his heart is. My worth is so much more than that." She explained. "That brings me back to the reason why I didn't show up that evening when I asked you to make a decision. I didn't want to replace Lauren only to end up in her shoes. Who's to say if you wouldn't have started messing with her behind my back. You know how shit is these days. The side chick becomes the main chick and somehow the main chick becomes the side chick."

"It wouldn't have been like that."

"Oh, yea? Because what I recall is you always saying that Lauren had been there way before me and that you had made a special commitment to her. However, you were finally going to break that commitment for little ole me? I don't think so. I'm still so confused though."

"Why?"

"How special is that commitment since you still ain't put a ring on it yet?"

"You really got jokes today, don't you?"

By: Tiece

"No, I'm just saying. Technically, I've been around for at least 7 years now. That's all."

Cain shook his head while glancing down at his cell phone, as an incoming text message chirped out loud. He opened the message.

What you doing baby? Thought you would've been home by now. LAUREN

I stopped by to see mom, but she ain't here. So, I'll be heading home shortly. CAIN

Okay. See you when you get here. LAUREN

Okay baby. CAIN

"Who was that, your woman?"

Cain nodded his head. "Yea."

"See what I mean."

Cain frowned. "What are you talking about?"

"I'm talking about you have a woman and she's probably wondering where you are. If that's the case then I know you didn't tell her you were here, because we don't even supposed to be operating like that anymore. Which tells me that you've not changed a bit, yet you're over here tripping about me getting married."

"Yea well, so." Cain said, like he was a 5 year old child. "Who is this nigga anyway?"

"He's my man and he'll be returning from overseas in a couple of months. We've been dating for two years now."

"And, you think two years is a long time? That ain't long enough for you to be seeing somebody, let alone getting ready to marry him."

"In your opinion, but I've known him much longer than two years. We actually went to school together. When we graduated, he enlisted in the Navy. We caught up through social media, started talking on the phone and he has flown me out to Germany a few times. Now, he'll be coming back home for at least 2 years and somewhere in that time we're gonna get married."

"I hope you don't think you're taking my daughter across seas to live with him."

"I never said that. Plus, I have a career here, my family is here and so that's not in the plans. However, if it was it wouldn't be none of your business."

"The hell you say. I don't want my daughter living miles and miles away from me."

"You sound like a real jackass Cain. You hardly ever spend time with her as is. That's why she don't care to go with you."

"She's knows her daddy, don't get it wrong. Plus, our relationship is a lot better since Lauren got involved."

Hazel scowled. "You sound stupid. Why should it have taken Lauren, mind you, your woman to get involved so you can get closer with your daughter? That should've been something that happened from the time she was born. That should've been the day you asked for a fucking DNA test!" she fussed.

"I wish you'd lighten up." Cain uttered, trying to calm the situation.

"Oh, now you want me to lighten up?"

"It doesn't have to be like this."

"Well, how should it be? Because I'm confused here. You have a woman. You should be going home to her right now, not standing in my face. Lauren is a good woman, if you don't want to be with her then you should tell her. But don't bring your ass over here in your feelings because now I'm moving on."

"First off, I never said I didn't want her."

"Then leave," Hazel said as she stood to her feet. "Navaeh isn't here, so you shouldn't be here either."

"What if I don't wanna leave?"

"Then I'll call Lauren and tell her to come get you and make you leave."

Cain stood there for a minute. He didn't have a chance in hell, especially since Hazel was now engaged to another. "It ain't gotta be like this."

"But it is. So, come on." She insisted, as Cain followed her to the front door. "I'll see you later."

Cain opened the door to walk out. He glanced back at Hazel with a sad expression on his face. He felt defeated, but knew he didn't run nothing when it came to Hazel. He shook his head, and then slowly headed back to his car. Hazel stood in the doorway until he was gone.

"I am so fucking blown right now I don't know what to do!" Lauren griped into the phone.

"What's wrong with you?" Tiana asked.

"I messaged Cain about an hour ago and asked him where he was and the bitch lied."

"What you mean by that?"

"He lied that's what I mean by that."

"Slow down Sis. How did you know he lied?" Tiana pondered, in a clueless, high-pitched tone.

"Because earlier, I spotted him driving through a green light, as I was sitting at the other one and something told me to follow him. So, I did. Needless to say, he ended up at Hazel's house and had been in there for a while. Instead of knocking on the muthafuckin' door like I started to do, I decided to text his black ass and ask what he was doing. Well, when he responded back, he said he was at his mama's house."

"Damn, he didn't say that did he?"

"Yea, while I'm sitting in my car watching his ass at her house."

"Wow, Sis. That's craaaazy. Maybe he had to stop by and see the baby right quick."

"Yea, but why lie about it? We don't do that, or at least he's not supposed to do that. Better yet, we're supposed to be better than that at this point."

"Yea, but it had to be an explanation right?"

"I guess not, unless it's one that would include them two fucking behind my back." Lauren said, as she searched for Cain's stash. He had moved his dope bag earlier that morning, but she was getting in the shower and didn't want to just stop what she was doing to watch him. The last thing she needed was for him to find out she'd been poppin' pills.

"You a'ight?"

"No."

"I think you need to sit down and breathe. It's not as serious as you think it is. You and Hazel have become cool. She doesn't seem like the type that would do that behind your back."

"How do you know? What is the type?" Lauren asked with sarcasm. "Maybe her calling me so we could get cool was really just so she could steal my man." She said as she discovered Cain's drug bag in the back of their closet.

Quickly, she grabbed it. Walked over to the bed and dumped all the contents in it on the bed. Cain had everything from Percocets, Molly's, E's, Vallum, and anything else on the market that made a bitch feel good. While continuing to discover the endless possibilities of the good shit, she pulled out a small ziplock bag of the white stuff also known as cocaine. She looked it over with eager eyes. Never had she gone this far or done anything so remotely absurd as trying a drug that she knew was completely off limits.

"What are you doing?" Tiana asked.

"Nothing," Lauren said, almost in a whisper.

"You're up to something. Are you high?"

"What you mean by high?" Lauren pondered while taking the ziplock bag of powder out of the bag of goodies.

"If you're asking what I mean by that, then that must mean you're on something else other than weed."

"No I'm not," Lauren quickly interjected. "I did smoke a joint right before calling you."

"You sure that's all you did?"

"Yea, I ain't done nothing else."

"Oh okay. I don't want you over there taking stuff because you might be in your feelings."

"I'm good, Sis. Yes, I'm pissed the fuck off, but I'm good."

"I think I need to come over there."

"No, just stay where you're at. I don't need a babysitter. I'm not doing anything that you need to be concerned about." She said, while opening the ziplock bag wanting to see if the white substance had a smell. Suddenly, the house alarm beeped in the background, startling her as she dropped the bag of powder on the floor. Cain was back, so quickly she started putting the goodies back in the bag.

"Hey, I gotta go. I'll call you back." Lauren said, while ending the call and sliding her cell phone in her pocket. She rushed to put the stuff back in the bag, and then hurriedly threw the bag back in the closet where she found it at.

As she headed out the bedroom, she turned to speed inside the master bathroom to clean herself up and check her face. Quickly, she closed the door shut behind her, followed by turning on the sink water.

"Aye Babe, where you at?" Cain called out, as he made his way into the bedroom.

By: Tiece

"I'm in here," Lauren answered, as thoughts of confronting him crossed her mind. Her phone rang causing her to jump. She pulled it out of her pocket to answer it. "I said I would call you back."

"Shit, I was making sure yo' ass hadn't jumped off a cliff." Tiana told her.

"Cain is back. That's why I said I'll call you back."

"Oh, okay. Where is he?"

"In the room."

"Where are you?" Tiana pondered.

"I'm in the bathroom." Lauren asked.

"You good in there Babe?" Cain called out.

"Yea, I'm good," she responded. "Be out in a minute."

"Damn, so you're going to front him?" Tiana asked.

"I don't know what to do. What you think I should do?"

"I don't think you should make a big deal out of nothing just yet. Try to feel the situation out first. You're a hot head, but you need to chill on this one. I don't think it's nothing you need to look into when it comes to Hazel and Cain." She said, just as her cell phone beeped of an incoming text message. "Sis, okay I won't do anything. YET," she added. "Gotta go."

"Alright." Tiana said.

If you're free tomorrow, I'd like to talk to you. HAZEL

Lauren frowned. "What the fuck?" she whispered. "I know this hoe ain't trying me."

When and what time? LAUREN

Fallin' In Love With The Goat 3

Around 1 at spin class if you're down. The Omni Gym on Wylds Road. I have day passes for friends. HAZEL

"Is this bitch serious, fucking spin class? Who the hell told her I like exercising? Furthermore, how the hell we gon' talk if we're exercising?"

"Babe, what you doing in there?" Cain asked.

"I'm coming." Lauren called out again, almost with an attitude. "Don't be fucking rushing me," she whispered, while washing her hands under the running water. After that, she messaged Hazel back.

Sure, I'll be there. LAUREN

Lauren exited the bathroom. She was already in her feelings and Hazel messaging her didn't make it any better. Not knowing if it was a set-up or not, she walked straight over to Cain who was sitting on the side of the bed holding the TV remote in his hand.

"Where were you earlier?"

Cain frowned. "Huh?"

"I didn't stutter." She quickly shot his way.

"What you mean where was I?" He asked.

"Exactly what I asked you. Do I need to rephrase it?"

"What's with the attitude?" Cain asked.

"Don't ask me a question with a question."

"I stopped by Mama's. Is that a problem now?" he pondered, feeling somewhat nervous inside, but keeping a straight, innocent face.

By: Tiece

Lauren stared him directly in the eyes. "You sure about that?"

"Uh, yea," he answered.

"Okay, that's all I need to know." She said, and turned to walk out the bedroom.

"Aye, what's the interrogation about?" he asked, with confusion written all over his face.

"If you don't know, then I don't either. I'll be sleeping in the guest room tonight." She told him and walked out the room with a mean expression.

"So, you just gon' walk out like that?"

"Sholl the hell is!" Lauren responded, and quickly disappeared.

"Man, she tripping!" Cain said in a low whisper. Lauren had him spooked. It was like she was telling him that she knew something without exactly saying that she knew something. "Damn," he irritably said while bending down to take off his shoes. His eyes landed on a white powder like substance that was on the floor. He drew a line through it with his finger to see what it was, but it led him to the ziplock bag half-filled with cocaine.

"What the fuck?!" He let out. A very bothered frown covered his face. He looked towards the door where Lauren had just walked out, and then back down at the content on the floor. Thoughts of her being in the bathroom for so long started to grow his suspicions. On top of that, her attitude sucked to the highest power. Something was definitely off with her and he wasn't going to stop until he found out exactly what her problem was.

Chapter Eleven

Jabari pulled up to the shop, he parked and then got out of his car. As he was walking up to the building Tonio was walking out the door. "Wassup Tonio?" Jabari said, as he gave the homey dap.

"Nothing much, B. Wassup with you?"

"Same ole, same ole." Jabari responded. "Did y'all get in some test runs today, because the rain coming tomorrow?"

"Yea, we got in a few."

"Okay, good. The race ain't for another 2 days, but it's supposed to rain all day tomorrow. It'll clear up by Sunday, but we don't do runs in the rain."

"Yea, I know." Tonio told him.

"Everything good though?"

"Yea, everything's good. The cars are revved up to go."

"Okay cool."

"We were just in there joking around and shit. But, my lady called acting like she miss me, so I'm gon' head on out."

"I feel you." Jabari grinned. "Bruno left already too? I don't see his ride out here."

"Yea, he only did a couple of runs and then he left. Your dad and Papers are gone for the day too."

"Yea, I talked to Pops on my way out here."

By: Tiece

"Cain and Justin in there though."

"Oh, okay cool." Jabari said, giving Tonio dap again. "Hold it down, Bruh."

"You too, B."

Jabari walked inside the shop to find his brother's still sitting around in the lobby area joking around. "Wassup y'all?"

"Wassup B," Justin said.

"Shit," Cain added.

Jabari grinned, as he walked over to sit down. "What y'all in here laughing about?"

"Justin might have to do the same you did." Cain said.

"What's that?"

"Knock a nigga out." He answered, as Jabari and Justin laughed out loud.

"I told that nigga he might have to do that." Jabari joked. "You had another run-in with him?"

"Nah, but I believe I might." Justin told him. "See, I've gone over to shawty's house twice this week—"

"Ohhh, so she's coming around now?" Jabari cut in.

"Yea, she said she was tired of putting her life on hold and so, she hit me up and wanted to try this thing again." He explained.

Cain nodded his head. "Ain't nothing wrong with that."

"So, anyway, while I been over there the nigga just keeps calling and calling. He'll call so much until she literally turns her phone off."

"Damn, he trippin," Jabari uttered.

"Same thing I be saying." Justin said. "I really think it's just control with this nigga. He be wildn' and shit, acting like he in his feelings but he's married with 2 other families on the side. She's one of them, and not the wife."

"Damn," Cain said. "Bruh, got it going on."

"Bruh USED to have it going on. Shyla ain't with that shit no more." Justin said, like he was taking up for his lady friend.

"He's the Clubs' owner right?" Cain asked.

"Yea, but technically she is now. He put 'em in her name. Some shit about his divorce with his wife, but he wants her to give 'em back to him when his divorce is final."

Jabari frowned. "That's some crazy shit."

"You telling me." Justin agreed. "I told her don't do it."

"No wonder the nigga acting crazy. That's exactly what he's probably thinking. If she moves on with somebody else, then she might start to have those kinds of thoughts. That man is just trying to protect his assets." Cain explained with a shrug.

"He better be trying to protect his ass before I beat the brakes off of him."

Cain and Jabari laughed.

"He keep asking for it." Cain chimed in.

"But nah, Bruh. Don't be fighting that nigga. Tell shawty to take out a restraining order out on him 1st. Then beat his ass afterwards. That way it'll be justified." Jabari told him.

Justin nodded his head. "You're right." He said. "I just hate for her to be going through all this. It's not that she can't hold her own because she's good with that, but he actually showed his gun at the event she was throwing Cashmere."

"Say what?" Cain scowled.

"And that's why she has to take out a restraining order. He don't seem like he's going to let up and I know you." Jabari said, just as Cain cut in.

"You be ready to beat a bitch ass." He said, with a shake of the head. "Yea, but I might have to shoot him."

"Do what you gotta do, Bruh." Jabari told him. "I just hope he get his shit together before it comes to anything like that."

"Yea, me too." Justin agreed. "One night I was over there and they was talking about you, Bruh. I told 'em they had to find something else to talk about. They can't just be dissing you like that in my face." He teased.

"What they were saying?" Jabari pondered.

"How you left Cashmere hanging at the gender reveal."

"I didn't leave her hanging—"

"I know," Justin laughed. "I was just playing. But, they did talk about the baby gender and how she wished you did come."

"Who, Cash?"

"Yea," Justin nodded.

"I had my reasons, but it looked like they were having a good time. Shyla sent me a video and a few of the pictures."

"So, what you gon' do about that situation, B?" Cain asked with curious eyes.

"If the baby is mine I'm gonna take care of her, if she's not then I don't know what to do."

"Why do you say that?" Cain asked.

"Because Slim was like a brother to me. If he was living I'd be his children's God-Father—"

"Well, maybe not in this case," Cain joked but was very serious.

"You know what I mean." Jabari said, giving his brother the side-eye. "Don't play nigga."

Cain grinned. "I'm just saying."

"Anyway," Jabari continued. "I know if the baby is Slick's she'll be spoiled by Trudy and their family. So, either way she won't want for nothing. But, at the end of the day she won't have a father in her life either. I've just been having thoughts of stepping up because maybe that's what I'm supposed to do. Slick would do it for me." He explained.

"I get your logic but I don't know. If that's the case, then maybe it's meant to set you free." Cain said.

"Maybe, but I don't feel like that right now, and until I do then I might be the one taking on that responsibility. It doesn't mean that I'm getting back with Cashmere, because I do know if that baby ain't mine then it's definitely a done deal with us. However, I don't want y'all to be shocked if I do step up to the plate."

"I commend you if you do. It takes a real man to do something like that. Most wouldn't give it a second thought." Justin said.

"I know, but then I'd have to tell Tiana about it. I don't really think she'll trip but do I even want to involve her in a situation like that?"

By: Tiece

"So, y'all getting serious?" Justin asked.

"I didn't say all that. We have been kicking it on a regular, but I think she wants more. I can understand if she does. I mean, she's a good woman with a nice career. She's very family oriented and in tune with my wants and needs. I don't believe she's fucking nobody else, but then again you never know," he said, with thoughts of how deceptive Cashmere was. "However, I think she's a different breed. The problem is I ain't in that head space right now. Not only am I fresh outta prison for a few months, but I'm fresh out of a relationship too. Mind you, a relationship that has given me the blues. Man, it's true what they say. We can dish the shit but we damn sholl can't take it. I ain't gon' lie. Cash broke me down. All the way down. How do you even trust another after that?"

"I don't know Bruh. If I had the answer to that we'd all be better in a better place." Cain answered.

"I know right," Justin agreed.

"So, what's up with you and YoYo?" Cain pondered.

"Nothing major," Jabari answered. "Ironically, it's one of the reasons why I like her so much. We enjoy each other's company whenever we kick it. There is no pressure or no additional attachments. It's just her and her career. She's a homebody and an overall good woman too, but she definitely has this bad girl image that turns me on. We haven't fucked yet, but I ain't pressed about that. It'll happen when it happens. I'm sure she's down, she just don't act like it."

"Sounds like there are 2 women falling in love with the Goat." Justin joked with laughter.

Fallin' In Love With The Goat 3

"Hell yea," Cain agreed. "But, I can see why you're taken by YoYo. It's definitely night and day when it comes to her and Sofia. "

"You ain't never lied. I'm feeling shawty though and I like the pace in which we're moving. It's pretty dope, ya know."

"That's wassup." Cain said, as he decided to take this as an opportunity to talk about his personal issues. "So, I didn't even want to mention this but what the hell. Maybe I can get some advice before I lose all my damn hair from worry."

"What's going on with you?" Justin asked.

"It's more like what's going on with Hazel and Lauren." Cain answered.

"Huh?" Jabari pondered with a curious expression. "We haven't really heard the name Hazel in a long time, especially in the same sentence as Lauren."

"I know because I try not to think about Hazel like that. Talk about a bitch breaking you down. Hell, that's what she did to me when she left me hanging."

"Yea, I remember that." Justin uttered. "Nigga was sick 'round here."

Jabari grinned with a shake of the head.

"Anyway, Hazel hits me up to tell me she's getting married, so I go over to her house and snap on her."

Jabari frowned. "Why? Don't you have a woman?"

"Yea, but that's besides the point."

"So, you say," Justin intervened.

"Anyway, I know I gotta accept that shit but I ain't like it."

By: Tiece

"And what does this have to do with Lauren?" Justin pondered.

"Lauren was acting funny as hell when I got home, so I was thinking that maybe Hazel called her and told her that I was over her house. See, when I was there she messaged me and I told her that I was visiting mama. But, when I got home she started questioning me like she knew better."

"And, that makes you think that Hazel told on you?"

"Yea, until I talked to her later. But before then, Lauren snaps on me and then walks out the room. Well, I bend down to take my shoes off and a bag of powder that came out of my duffle bag was open and on the floor."

"What now?!" Jabari asked in a high-pitched tone. Back up a lil bit. I'm confused like a muthafucka. You got too much shit going on."

"I agree." Justin said.

"Long story short, I found a bag of coke on the floor. I think Lauren been in my shit."

"Been in your shit and doing what?"

"Using it." He admitted.

The brother's frowned with concern in their eyes. "Nah, you must have that wrong." Jabari said.

"I wish. See, after I spotted the coke, I went inside the closet and grabbed my duffle bag. I went through my shit and sure enough I was missing pills. Mostly, my Ecstacy pills."

"So, you think she's poppin' pills?"

Fallin' In Love With The Goat 3

Cain hunched his shoulders. "It's possible and maybe she's graduating to something stronger."

Jabari shook his head. "I don't know about that one Bruh."

"I'm telling you, her behavior has been totally different these past couple of months. At first, I was just enjoying the ride. I thought she was stepping up her game like I'd been asking for years, but it hit me the minute I noticed I had some shit missing."

"You know that's serious right?" Justin asked him.

"Hell yea, and especially if she's using coke. I know I haven't drove her to that point."

"I hope not, but she's been acting funny all week. Hell, last night she stayed with Tiana." Cain said. "Strange thing is that I spoke with Hazel and she said that they were supposed to meet earlier in the week, but Lauren didn't show."

"Damn, she onto something. I don't know what, but for her to be acting like that, she's pissed off."

"I know right." He said, glancing down at his cell phone as it chirped of an incoming text message.

I'm parked at the coffee shop waiting to meet Lauren. She messaged me not long ago. I told her I'd meet her after work. Do you know what this is about, since she flaked on me earlier this week? HAZEL

I don't know, but hit me up the minute it's over. CAIN

Okay I will. HAZEL

"What the fuck?!" Cain said, now scratching in his head, feeling some type of way.

By: Tiece

"What?!" Justin quickly asked.

"That was Hazel. She said Lauren wanted to meet up and talk."

"Didn't she just skip out on her earlier this week?" Jabari asked.

"Yea, so I don't know what this is about." Cain said with a shake of the head. "It's too late for her to be acting crazy now. I know I ain't doing nothing with Hazel."

"What about the other baby mama?" Justin asked with curious eyes.

"All Sofia do is suck my dick from time to time and I nut in her mouth. I get my boy and go on about our business."

"Damn, you don't think she said something do you?" Jabari asked.

"Nah, she been cool as a fan lately. I highly doubt she's said anything. Her and Lauren don't even talk like that, PERIOD."

"Oh, okay. Well, I don't know what it is."

"Me either." Justin said.

Jabari's wandering thoughts took him to a whole new head space, and then swiftly he changed the subject. "So, what y'all think about Pops bugging Bruno's car and his house?" he asked.

"I think if it's something there, he will definitely find out that way. Bruno's bound to break or say something incriminating." Justin said.

"It's just so hard to believe that he could be in on anything dealing with Slick's death. They were so close." Cain said.

"Bruno's been playing us. I have a feeling it's been longer than we thought. Unfortunately, Leo don't want to meet up with me now, so that's not helping us at all. For Slick to say this man was closely in our circle and for him to mention that Leo said something about the dude being into race cars too, was the biggest hint of them all to me. So, I believe it's him."

"Damn, that's fucked up if it is." Justin said. "But what would he have to do with Skylar's death? Or is it even related?"

"It has to be because Leo was talking about Mars when he mentioned it to Slick. So, something is definitely off. I don't know. I'm still so confused; especially when it comes to Skylar." Jabari explained with a shake of the head.

"Damn, I hate that nigga skipped town like that. It had to be something for him to come forward after all this time, and then suddenly just disappear again. Like what's his motive? What's the point? Is Mars with him just laying low and fucking with us? Like what is it? I don't fucking get it either."

Jabari shrugged. "I don't know but we can't stop here. Everything is going to unfold and when it does, it's going to hit us hard. All I can say is prepare yourselves, because I can feel a storm coming and it ain't nothing we can do to stop it."

Cain's cell phone chirped again. "I hope this ain't more bullshit." He said, glancing down at the phone. Ironically, it was a text message from Bruno with a video attached. "Speaking of the devil."

"Who Bruno?" Justin pondered.

"Yea, he just sent me a Youtube video. He said that Ace is calling you out."

Jabari frowned. "Ace? Let me see that." But before Cain could hand him his phone, Jabari's phone alerted him of 2 messages back to back. "Never mind, I'm sure he's sending it to me now." He said looking at his phone. "Him and Tonio."

The brother's wasted no time pressing play on the video to see what all the hype was about.

"Yo, yo, yooooo! This is yo' homey Ace in full effect. I heard The Goat was back!" he chuckled in the video. "I've been waiting for the homey to call me out, but I guess he ain't ready for this smoke. Or, maybe he think I went into retirement for good." He laughed, while smoking his blunt. "Naaaaaah, my nigga, Ace is back and I want ALL the Smoke! Where's the Goat?" he said looking around as his crew laughed in the background. "I see you've been spanking ass on the strip, but you still ain't faced me yet. Your crew is racing Sunday. I'll be in your City. I'm calling you out now! What you gon' do?" he asked with a smug smile plastered across his face. "Somebody find that nigga and tell him Ace is looking for him." He grinned. "Ace is back! Ace is back! Ace is back!" he laughed, and then the video ended.

The brother's looked at each other. Cain grinned with a shake of the head. Seeing that video seemed like it gave him an unexplainable rush inside.

"Oh Shit!! I've been waiting for this." He said, and then looked over at Jabari.

"Yea, Bruh. What you gon' do?" Justin asked. "I think it's time you show you this cat what you're made of."

"Cain, bring my whip round front." Jabari told him, speaking of his race car. "We 'bout to get in some test runs before this rain comes through."

Fallin' In Love With The Goat 3

"Yeeessss!" Cain shouted, as he quickly got up and headed to the back of the shop.

"I'll call Pops," Justin said. "History is about to go down!"

By: Tiece

Chapter Eleven

"Wassup Sis, you good?" Tiana asked, as she entered the guest room and sat on the bed next to Lauren.

Lauren shook her head. "Look at me. Do I look good?" she asked.

"Do you really want me to answer that?" Tiana teased to try and lighten her sister's load. "What do you wanna do tonight since we're not going to the track?"

"I don't know. I'm sorry that you're here with me, because I know you want to see Jah's big race."

"I do, but you come first and without you there, I'd be lost girl." She grinned.

"I feel bad that I'm not there to support Jabari and the crew, but I feel it's for the best. I know Cain is there and I'm not ready to talk to him yet."

"I feel you." Tiana said. She felt bad for her, because she was really going through a rough time. "For what it's worth, I think you're a really strong person. You just don't give yourself enough credit. It takes a woman that knows her worth to walk away from a bad situation, no matter how much time you've put in."

"It still hurts though."

"I know it does, but you're not doing anything wrong. Cain is the one that's losing out, not you."

Fallin' In Love With The Goat 3

"I knew he was a cheater, but I didn't know he would do me like that." Lauren said with a shake of the head.

"And just to think at one point I was really trying to give him the benefit of the doubt. I even had the nerve to make nice with Hazel only to find out she had a 4 year affair with the bastard and then got pregnant afterwards."

"I couldn't believe she came clean with all that tea. I'm sure Cain is pissed the fuck off with her."

"Who gives a fuck how he feels? She didn't have a choice," Lauren said. "After I confronted her ass about him being over her house that day, she just told it all. Maybe I had pissed her off by talking shit like I wanted to beat her ass or maybe she felt bad for me and wanted me to see the nigga for who he really was. Either way, she opened my eyes to some real shit."

"Yea, she did that." Tiana agreed.

"I just can't believe that he played me like that. And, according to her his ass was going to leave me for her."

"You believe that?"

"Hell yea, because back then he definitely started acting different. I wasn't a fool, so I knew something was up with him. However, I never thought he'd be so in love with the next bitch that he was thinking about leaving me."

Tiana shook her head. "That's that bullshit right there."

"You telling me." Lauren uttered.

"Sis, I was going through some shit; especially after finding out about Cain's 2nd baby. That did something to my soul. I started taking his pills and shit trying to feel better. And, don't get me wrong, it worked. I felt good, stayed horny, and put on a fake front that I was in a better space, but I was far from that. Shit, still is. I knew shit had gotten real after I caught him over to Hazel's house and he lied about it. Remember when I was on the phone with you that night?"

"Yea, you lost your damn mind." Tiana commented.

"I did, but I knew I was gone when I found his stash bag and was tempted to try coke."

Tiana frowned. "Coke like a soda? Or coke like cocaine, powder?"

"The latter." Lauren admitted.

"Wow, you gotta be kidding me Sis."

"I wish I was. Shit had me gone." Lauren confessed. "That's why I had to snap out of it. I've been with Cain way too long to keep putting up with his shit. Hell, for all I know he could still be fucking Sofia. Shit he can get Cannon anytime he wants now. Not that I have anything against his lil cute butt, but I definitely ain't feeling his daddy like that. I don't trust the bitch."

"And with good reason." Tiana agreed. "I'm just glad that you got ahold of yourself before you went down that dark path. At the end of the day, it's not worth it. Men can do whatever they want to a woman, hurt their feelings, cheat, talk shit and all, and we still put up with it. There comes a day when somebody gotta be the smart one about it and let it go. I told myself that I didn't want to waste years or even months on a nigga ever again if I already see that our relationship ain't leading in the direction it should be going in."

"That's why I'm done with Cain. There is nothing more precious than time and I've wasted a lot of that on an ungrateful ass nigga. Maybe some of our problems stemmed from me and the way I am and if so, I can live with that. What he took for granted another man will love. All I know is that I'm not wasting a whole lot of time trying to figure it out no more. When they show me who they are the 1st time, I'm gonna believe 'em and move the fuck on."

Tiana grinned, but nodded her head to definitely agree. "Giiiirl, you ain't never lied which brings me to Jabari. I never thought I'd find myself falling in love with the Goat, but I am."

"Awww, that's sweet." Lauren said with a smile.

"No, the fuck it ain't sweet either." Tiana quickly said, causing Lauren to shoot her the side-eye followed by a loud laugh. "No, but I'm serious. Jabari is the coolest, sweetest person I've ever met. He's down to earth, he comes through when I need him and he can fuck like no other. Not to mention how fine his ass is. Shit and he's handsome as hell."

Lauren frowned, with an irritated expression. "Okay bitch, what's the problem then?"

"The problem is that he's not ready for me. Not only that, but he's also seeing Sofia's sister. I mean, they aren't fucking I don't believe. At least that's what he told me and I believe him. He doesn't have a reason to lie, but he did admit to liking her. I can respect that, but at the same time I don't want to be a part of that. He tells me that he's not ready to be in a relationship with anybody right now. He just wants to live and I can't blame him."

"At least he's honest. Gotta respect that." Lauren commented.

By: Tiece

"And you're right. He's fresh out of an unhealthy relationship, on top of just getting out of prison. I can respect what he tells me because most men won't do that. They'll just try to play you. But, I'm not in that head space. I would like him all to myself and I know that's not going to happen. He may have a change of heart one day, but how long will that take? Is it my obligation to just sit around and wait?"

"Nope," Lauren answered. "Ask me, I had to learn the hard way. Hell, almost 12 years and I still ain't got a ring on my finger. The shit ain't worth it."

"I believe you," Tiana said. "Well, I did call him and wish him luck on his race. I apologized for not being there, but he understood. I guess I'll enjoy his company for the time being, but I don't have any expectations whatsoever. I'm not setting myself up for the okie doke," she joked with laughter. "Now on another note, Derek called me. He wants to stay here for a couple weeks. His house sold quicker than he thought and he has to be out by the end of the month."

"So, are you going to let him come?"

"Ashley is stoked and says I should. You know she'll do anything to have her father around."

Lauren shook her head. "I know." She grinned.

"But, I don't know. I'm still thinking about it." Tiana said. "He need not think it's going to be more than that and he definitely will have a timeframe of when his ass needs to be gone."

"Well, look at it this way. He drives trucks, so he'll hardly be here anyway. He does look out, and he is good to his daughter. Maybe you should, just for a couple of weeks."

Fallin' In Love With The Goat 3

"I'll think about it." Tiana said, as she laid back on the bed. "Bitch, what you wanna do now? I'm not staying cooped up in this room with yo ass!"

Biggs and Papers pulled up to the track, but didn't immediately enter or get out. They parked along the back entrance overlooking the exciting mayhem going on before them, as the cars were lined, people cheering and chanting, and food vendors packed and making money. The crowd was thick and loud to say the least, as people waited to see the last race of the night between Ace and Jabari.

Papers smiled. "I can remember back when we would bring out crowds like this. You were the Goat back then and still is."

Biggs smled. "Yea, those were the days. It feels good to be still living my dream through him. I'm overly excited and just as ready for this race as everybody else."

"Shit, me too." Papers agreed with a huge smile on his face. "You think nephew is ready for tonight?"

"He better be. We got a whole lot riding on this one. Not only have we put bucks on him, but he can't afford to lose after the last 2 runs against Ace."

"I must admit, the kid is definitely good." Papers said, speaking of Ace. "Him and nephew have some of the same rituals before a race."

"Yea, I been peeped that. They both say small prayers, and toss up coins before they race. They move in similar ways as well. You know Jabari is real laid-back and nonchalant. Ace has that same demeanor. "

"I believe Ace has watched nephew so much over the years that he now mimics everything he does. I think so much so, that it threw B off his game the first time they raced and it seemed like it threw him off twice."

Biggs grinned.

"Shit, I'm for real. Losing twice to the same cat is unbelievable; especially for him. You never lost a race, at least not one that counted," he slid in.

"Yea, but Jah was just off his game," Biggs said, taking up for his son. "It happens, but tonight I have a feeling he's ready. I believe it. I saw it in his eyes. Plus, his car is on the line and he ain't going out like that."

"Yea, I forgot about that." Papers agreed with a nod of the head. "He definitely ain't going out like that. At least I would hope not," he added, but then moved on in another direction. "On the other hand, Tonio is turning heads and learning how to hold the steering wheel a lot better. I love how he pulled out slower, but came out with a win in the end. Looks like the number one Stunner is looking more like the number three or four now."

Biggs laughed. "You ain't lyin'," he joked. "I'm proud of Tonio, but Bruno is looking more and more suspicious. Where was his head during the race? He let Roy spank his ass like it was nothing."

"Right and I have never seen him lose a race like that. It was straight blowout." He said, thinking back at the live video they had watched of both races.

"Me either," Biggs agreed. "So, what have you caught on the bug yet?"

"Nothing, and I don't know if we will." Papers answered.

"I didn't hear much either when I listened in. I'm hoping we're wrong about him, but things just keep coming up and the reason we never peeped it because he was NEVER a suspect. I'll be making a trip to California soon. You're welcome to ride if you want to."

"You know I'm tagging along." Papers said. "Who are we going to see?"

"Leo. Mar's cousin," he responded. "I put my P.I. on it and have everything I need, including his address. I just needed a lead. Once I got that, I wasn't worried about him meeting up with my son, because I'll be meeting up with him sooner rather than later."

"I like the sound of that."

"We'll get closure one way or the other and if Bruno is involved in any of this, he's going to wish like hell he wasn't."

A light knock on the driver window of the truck caught Biggs attention, as he looked to the side. Blinking twice, and then twice again, he slowly let the window down.

"Gemma?" Biggs said in a light, high-pitched tone like he was somewhat unsure, but from the look in his eyes he was definitely sure.

"Hi Samuel," Gemma pleasantly said with a sweet smile on her face.

"Wow, it's been a long time." Biggs said, still with a shocked expressed.

By: Tiece

"Yes, it has been way too long. Hello Sebastian," she said, looking past Biggs and at Papers.

"Gemma, how are you?"

"I'm blessed, can't complain." She responded.

"Samuel can we chat for a second?"

Biggs looked over at Papers. "You got time. I'll pull the car out the trailer and drive it around to the strip."

"Okay cool, but don't y'all start the race without me being there."

"We won't." Papers responded, as he got out of the truck.

Biggs looked at Gemma. "Sure, get in." he told her.

Once inside the truck, Gemma nervously smiled. "You're still looking good."

"Not better than you. You haven't changed a bit." Biggs told her.

"Thanks, you haven't either."

"I see you're still into fast cars," he joked.

"It's always been a love of mine. I guess you can blame that on my father. The need for speed is in our blood." She told him.

"Yea, had it not been for him we never would've met." Biggs told her. "Your father was a man I looked up to in the drag racing arena. He was one of the best ever."

"You were too, though. Don't forget that." Gemma told him.

"Well," Biggs said with a cocky, playful smile. "You're right." He teased.

Gemma laughed. "Still got that sense of humor too."

"And you still have that beautiful smile," he told her. Just sitting with her brought back memories of way back. She was someone that he'd become really close with, a woman that held as much or even more interest in the world of racing than he did. She was once a really good friend of his and they shared some of the most intimate moments ever and he could never forget them.

"Oh, wow, I got so caught up in seeing you that I haven't even expressed how awful I felt to hear about your father. How is he?"

"He's a fighter, so he's trying his best not to show us a weak side. It's just not in his blood. So, he's decided to leave us in a week, as his farewell to us all."

"Huh? I don't understand."

"He wants to die in peace and in the eyes of his personal nurse and my mom. He doesn't want us around to see him go through any pain. He doesn't want us to remember him like that. Since he has refused to take chemo treatments the cancer is slowly spreading. We can't tell that he's even ill or in pain, because he's still fixing on cars and revving up the engines every day."

Biggs smiled. "That's wassup." He expressed from a soft spot he had in his heart for the legendary dragster. "I would've loved to see him again. So, when you talk to him tell him I asked about him and I wish him nothing but peace and joy on his journey."

"I will." Gemma smiled.

"So, what brings you to Georgia? Are you recruiting new drivers?"

"No, I'm just here to watch the race."

"Yea, my son is up next." Biggs told her.

By: Tiece

"Oh, I know your son quite well. We've followed his career since he first got on the scene. Reminded me from the start of my own son. He loves racing, as well. It's definitely in his bloodline. He'll be racing tonight too."

Biggs frowned a little. "He's racing tonight. It's only one race left." He said, as he stared into Gemma's eyes.

"My son is Ace." She confessed, with a nervous smile on her face. "You'll be watching both of your son's race against each other tonight."

"What?!" Biggs let out in an uncertain tone. "Ace is what?"

"Ace is your son Samuel." She admitted.

Biggs sat silently with thoughts rumbling through his mind. The last thing he was expecting to hear was that Ace was his son. He shook his head in disbelief. "You can't be serious."

"Oh, but I am." She told him.

"Why now?" Biggs asked, almost with instant tears in his eyes. "Why now Gemma?"

"I had no choice. My father is dying and because of the close relationship he and Ace share it's going to tear him apart. He wants to be strong for me, but deep down inside I know it's eating him up. Four years ago, Ace lost the only man he knew as his father, which was my husband from a senseless murder. My father helped fill that void. He practically helped me raise Ace, so there was a solid bond already there which also helped in his grievance process, because dad always made sure he was good and tunneled his energy into what he loved to do."

"That was racing." Biggs cut in.

Fallin' In Love With The Goat 3

"Yes, but he called himself went into retirement. Even though he told everyone that it was because of your son's absence. However, he was hiding behind the truth of losing his father."

"Wow," Biggs let out. "How did I not know that? The world knows your father. I don't know how I missed him at the last 2 races. Where was he? Why he didn't come over? Does he know that Ace is my son, is that why he stayed away?"

"Well, my father was never in the forefront when it came to Ace and his races. Even on social media he stays away from the cameras. It has nothing to do with you. He just wanted to stay out of the spotlight for a change. He wanted Ace to make a name for himself without people automatically feeling like he was entitled. He's never been on camera with his grandson publicly. However, they have many private memories, photos, and videos together."

"I'm sure," Biggs nodded.

"Wow," he said again for the umpteenth time. "Do Ace know anything? I mean, does he know that we once had an affair?"

"No, I never told him. But I do think it's past time. I need for him to know his real family, to know his real father. I do have 3 daughters by my husband. One is Ace's camerawoman." She grinned. He does have 3 other sisters, by me and my husband, but he deserves more. It's his right to know and I regret withholding it from him. I'm sorry I kept it from you too. I know how close you are with your sons."

"Yes, I'm very close with them and now I feel like I've missed out on so much of his life."

"I know, it's been over 30 years." She said.

By: Tiece

"That's a long time Gemma. How do we get past that?" he said, just as his cell chirped of an incoming message. He looked down to read it.

I know you're enjoying memory lane but the race is nearing. You might wanna wrap it up. PAPERS

I'm coming. BIGGS

"We don't. We just try our best to make up for it." She answered. "He's probably going to hate me for a while, but he'll get over it. I just wanted you to know because I'll be telling him tonight as well. I think he's trying to move to Georgia after the revelation that my father has come up with."

"Moving to Georgia?" Biggs asked with a perplexed expression.

"Yes, I think. So, maybe it's a move for the better. What made him choose Georgia I have no clue, but if this is where his heart leads him then so be it. I approve of his choices."

"I still can't believe it. Ace is my son. You sure about that?" he pondered.

"I'm positive, just look at him. The resemblance is there and very strong. You just had no reason to see it, but I'm sure you will after tonight." She explained. "It's true, we had a cute lil romance that lasted long enough for us to conceive him. We definitely had a thing for each other, but you wanted your wife back. And, when I found out I was pregnant, I took my ass back home. There I found out I was pregnant, but I married two years later. However, my husband had been in Ace's life since he was born."

"Wow, this feels like a dream."

Fallin' In Love With The Goat 3

"I know it does, but I need you to know this." She said, just as her cell phone alerted her of an incoming text message. She looked down to read it.

Ma where you at? The race is starting soon. ACE

I'm coming Love. GEMMA

"Well, I guess that's my queue. Ace is messaging that the race is about to start."

"Yea, Papers messaged me too." Biggs said. "So, will I see you again?"

"Yes, we're here for a few days. I would like for us to meet up somewhere, so we can talk. All of us." She told him.

"That's fine. I'd like that." Biggs told her. "He reached in the middle console and came out with one of his business cards. "Just call me and let me know when."

"Okay, I will." Gemma said, and with that she got out of the truck and disappeared in the crowd of people.

Biggs sat lost in thought, but he knew he had to shake it off. His son was about to have one of the most anticipated races of all time. Shockingly, it was against his brother.

By: Tiece

Chapter Twelve

"Aye Pops, where you been?" Jabari asked, as he walked over. "This shit is about to get real."

Biggs laughed. "I know son, you got this." He said, just as Ace made his way.

"The legendary Goat is in the house," Ace said, with a smile and a handshake. "It's always pandemonium when me and this guy get together." He said, pointing over Jabari.

"Yes, it is, but it's great to finally meet you." Biggs said with a smile. He could definitely see the resemblance now. How did he not see that before?

"Yea, I was just telling B that I had to meet you this time. I wasn't leaving the city until I did." He joked but was very serious. "I just want you to know that I think you're one of the greatest to ever do it, along with grandfather," He added. "You're definitely been an inspiration and it's such a thrill to be racing your son."

Biggs smiled. "It's an honor to finally meet you." He told him. "Y'all ready?"

"About as ready as I'll get." Jabari told him. "Question is, are you ready?" He asked Ace. "Pops I hope we got room in the trailer because I'm taking his car home with me tonight."

Ace laughed out loud. "In your dreams," he said with a shake of the head. "You getting this shit, Sis." He said to his camerawoman.

"Yes," the cute girl grinned, as she continued to record. "Ma!" Ace called out. "Over here."

Gemma walked over and gave her son a hug.

"Meet B and his dad—"

"I've met Samuel before. Remember I told you we met years ago?" she said.

"That's right, I forgot. Well, this is his son, The Goat Jr. The one I'm gonna spank tonight." He grinned. "See, I have my good luck charm here." He told Jabari. "She rarely makes an appearance to my races, so be prepared for this loss."

Jabari laughed. "Nice to meet you, ma'am."

"Call me Gemma," she insisted. "And, it's nice to meet you too."

"Aye, y'all need to get ready," Papers said, as he intercepted their conversation. "You ready nephew?" he pondered, but gave Biggs the side-eye, like he knew it was something more going on than just a pop up visit from Gemma.

Jabari and Ace headed out to their cars. "You sure you ready for this?" Ace asked Jabari.

Jabari grinned. "Yup!"

Ace laughed, as he walked up to his car. It was a shiny, candy painted black, 1967 Chevy II with a 6.2 LS engine that was rumbling loud as hell like it was trained to go. The windows were darkly tinted, to a point that it was hard to see inside the car. Ace pulled out his lucky coin and kissed it. He threw it up in the air, as it landed in his hand. Whatever it landed on, only he knew as he smiled at his opponent, and then got in his car.

By: Tiece

Jabari stood by his car. It was funny to see Ace have the same ritual as him. He pulled out his lucky coin, but the 2 times he raced Ace it landed on tails and he lost. As he contemplated what he would do, tossing the coin wasn't one of them. It was the first time since he'd began racing professionally that he wasn't going to toss his coin. The last thing he wanted was for it to land on tails, because he was not backing out of this race for nothing or nobody. Instead, he kissed his 2 fingers and held them high to the sky. A race wouldn't be a race without showing his respects to Skylar, Slick and the most High. They weren't there in body, but they were there in spirit cheering him on.

He glanced back at his crew, giving them a thumbs up and then waving to the loud crowd of people that was chanting his name. He spotted his nephew in the crowd, sporting his lil Mickey Mouse Beats on his ears. He couldn't help but smile. Then he spotted Cashmere sitting next to Shyla. He didn't even know she was there, but it felt good to see her face. She smiled at him and waved her hand in the air. He waved back with a nod of the head, and then got inside of his car.

As always, Jabari said a silent prayer and imagined Slick sitting over in the passenger seat. "You ready for this win, Bruh?" he said to Slick, as if he were going along for the ride.

Jabari glanced over to the side of him, as Ace revved up his car for show. Everything was on the line, money, pride, reputation, and his car. Losing wasn't in the cards, so he definitely had to make sure to not come up short. As the flag dropped, Jabari pressed the pedal to the metal and sped down the strip wide ass open. Off to the side he could see Ace, it looked like they were neck in neck. Down the strip they went, reaching speeds of 100 plus, but it felt like it was moving in slow motion. Tunnel vision set in and the only thing ahead was the finish line. He wasn't sure where the surge of HP came from, but suddenly it kicked into gear and as Jabari walked off from Ace by an inch or two, he skirted across the winning line.

The crowd went wild the minute Jabari stepped out of his car. It was pure love and emotions running high, as everyone cheered and chanted, "The Goat is back!" Jabari smiled, and a satisfied smile on his face. He had definitely come back in a big way and proved to everyone why he was the Goat. The crew ran over to him, jumping around and yelling. Cain hugged him tight, followed by Jabari then Papers.

"You did it Bruh!" Justin yelled.

"It was your time tonight B and you did that!" Cain grinned with joy. He was excited and very happy for his brother.

"I'm proud of you nephew," Papers said. The whole crew was happy.

Biggs stood back feeling proud of his son, but couldn't help thinking about his other son.

Ace got out of his car, with a smile on his face. It was the 1st race he'd ever lost, but he didn't mind losing to someone like Jabari. He walked over and held out his hand to shake his opponents. "Good race, good race." He said, with a friendly hug. "Congratulations."

"I appreciate that, homey." Jabari said. "It was a good race."

Biggs walked over and congratulated both men. He hugged Jabari, and then Ace. It was a proud moment for him, rather bittersweet too. A part of him just wanted to come out say what he'd just learned but he knew in his heart that he had to wait. Gemma had to smooth things over first, because the last thing he'd ever want a child of his to know was that he turned his back on them. Truth is that he never knew he existed, but from that night forward he was going to be sure to make up for lost time. He just hoped that Ace would let him.

After the race had died down, and people were getting in their cars and leaving, Cashmere was approached by Jabari as she sat on the bleachers tying up her shoe.

"You need help with that?" he asked with a friendly smile.

Cashmere looked up and smiled back. "Nah, I got it."

"Looks like you were having a lil trouble over here. Thought I'd come rescue you."

Cashmere laughed. "Well, this baby is definitely getting in the way of things that I used to take for granted."

"I'm sure," Jabari laughed, as he sat down beside. "So, how are you?"

"I'm good, never better." She answered. "And you?"

"I'm good." He nodded.

"That's good. Congratulations on your win. You had me sitting on the edge of this bleacher. I mean, y'all were neck in neck at one point and then you just hit the juice on him."

Jabari grinned. "The juice?"

"Yep," Cashmere laughed.

"Where's Shyla? I thought I saw her here earlier."

"She just left with Justin. You know I don't cock block, so I told her I didn't mind driving back home."

Jabari grinned. "You crazy."

"I'm for real." She said. The conversation was cool but it definitely felt a little weird being that they hadn't been talking or even in that space.

"The gender reveal was nice. I had Shyla send me some of those pictures. It was beautiful and I knew you were having a girl."

"You didn't know nothing," Cashmere laughed.

"I told you." Jabari teased with a nod of the head.

"I'm actually glad it's a girl. I can't wait to meet her and teach her to be a better woman than I am."

"You're not that bad." Jabari told her.

"Yes, I am. I've done some things that I'm not proud of. I used to be mad at you for the way you were treating me but I can't blame you. There aren't enough sorry's in the world that I could give you to let you know how sincere I am about hurting you. I truly apologize for my behavior."

"I appreciate the apology but we can move on from that now. I'm just glad you're in a much better head space and hopefully, we can be cordial parents if that's in the cards for us. Either way, I wanted you to know that I'll be there for her if it's Slick's baby. I won't turn my back on her. The truth is that Slick is gone, but I know he'd still want me to be a part of his daughter's life. Especially since he can't be here to raise her himself. We'll probably never get back together. I know people say, never say never, but sometimes we just have to accept what is and to let go of the hurt."

By: Tiece

"I agree." Cashmere said. "Good thing for me is that I finally started to see things that way. We're in this predicament because of me and I fully accept that. I also accept the fact that I need to move on and allow myself to heal and grow from this, as well."

Jabari smiled, as he leaned in for a hug. Cashmere hugged him back.

"For the record," she added. "I know you'll still be here for her if the baby is Slick's, but I don't ever want you to feel like that's something you gotta do."

"Look, I wouldn't be doing nothing I don't wanna do. However, I'll be doing this for my homey and for her because he's not here."

"I understand." Cashmere said, as she stood to her feet. "Well, the cars have thinned out. I guess that's my queue to leave now."

"It was good talking to you." Jabari said.

"Same here," Cashmere said. She walked off, heading in the direction of her car. Any other time she'd be sick on her stomach and in her feelings from what Jabari had said to her. But not this time. She was getting stronger by the day and it was all because of her baby.

As she walked up to her car, she sighed with a shake of the head as her eyes widened. "Not tonight!" she irritably said, kicking the front flat tire. "How the fuck did that happen?" she pondered to herself while pulling her cell phone from her pocket. The parking lot wasn't quite empty but she didn't know anybody there. She thought about calling Shyla, but just as she started to, someone called out to her.

"Aye, you okay?" Ace asked, as he pulled up beside her.

"Not really," Cashmere responded with an irritated expression.

Ace parked his car and then got out. "Looks like you ran over a nail," he said while examining the tire. "My homey can change that for you." He said, pointing back at the truck that was following him. "Aye Wiz, park next to me and come here." He called out.

"You don't have to do this for me." Cashmere said.

"Nonsense, you think I can pass by a pretty lady like yourself and not help her when she's in need? I'm not that type of guy." He told her.

Cashmere smiled. "Thank God." She uttered, causing Ace to smile.

She grabbed the side of her stomach and took in a deep breath.

"You okay?" Ace asked with concerned eyes.

"Yea, I'm just ready to get home. This little one must feel just as agitated as I do." She said, just as Jabari pulled up.

He let his window down with curious eyes. "You okay Cash?"

"I just got a flat tire." she responded. "Oh, I can change that for you."

"Well," Cashmere said, as she looked over at Ace. "He's going to help me with it, so you can go. But, thank you B." She said with a smile.

"You got her homey?" Jabari asked, as he looked at Ace. A part of him wanted to get out, but he didn't want to overstep his boundaries if she didn't need him to.

"Yea, she's in good hands." Ace told him.

"A'ight, y'all have a good night." Jabari said, and with that he pulled off.

Cashmere could tell that he didn't like it, but what could he do about it? He had not long ago made it very clear that he had no interest in getting back with her and she was fine with that. It was something she had certainly come to terms with.

"I thought I knew who you were." Ace chimed in with a lightbulb moment. "It's been awhile since I last saw you. Not that we were ever in a close up space like we are now." he added. "But you and B were a couple once upon a time. I take it that's not the case no more."

"Your take is on point." She answered.

"Hey," Wiz spoke as he walked over.

"Hey," Cashmere spoke back.

"Can you pop your trunk so I can grab the spare?"

"Sure," Cashmere said, as she popped the trunk for him. She grabbed the side of her stomach again, and then took another deep breath.

"You sure you're okay?" Ace pondered.

"Yea, this happens from time to time. I'm just ready to go home and lie down." She told him.

"Let me take you home. I'll have Wiz change the tired, and Barry can drive your car home."

"Who is Barry?" Cashmere asked.

"My other homey. He's riding in the car with me."

"You got a lot of homey's." Cashmere joked.

Fallin' In Love With The Goat 3

"They're also a part of my crew." He told her. "So, is your car in the back of the trailer or did you give it up already?"

Ace laughed, "You got jokes?"

"Noooo," Cashmere laughed. "I was just asking."

"It's in the trailer. B told me to keep it for our next race."

"Well, that was dope of him." Cashmere said.

"I guess, but I would've taken his ride for sure."

Cashmere laughed.

"So, you gonna let me take you home?"

"No, but you don't have to go out of your way for me."

"Nonsense," he told her. "I'll be in the city for a few more days anyway. I don't mind. It'll give me something to do. Plus, you can fill me in a little more as to what you got going on these days. Well, besides being pregnant." He teased. "It ain't his baby is it?"

"It's a looong story." She told him.

"Well, we got time." Je grinned, while opening his car door. "Barry, I need you to drive her car for me. Wiz is changing the tire, but when he's done, drive it to the address that I'm going to send you."

"It must be nice." Cashmere said.

"If you keep talking to me you find out just how nice." he responded.

By: Tiece

Chapter Thirteen

Cashmere sat on the bed in Indian style, folding the pretty outfits that she'd gotten for the baby. She had her music bumping in the background and was in a really chill headspace.

Shyla entered the bedroom. "Oh my Gooooosh! Bestie every time I see you there is this glow-up that I'm so very proud of. You're big and round now."

"Almost about to pop." Cashmere uttered.

"Yea, but you're 30 weeks along. You don't have much time left. She'll be here before we know it."

"Where does the time go?" Cashmere asked.

"It definitely goes by fast, that's for sure."

"So, why are you all dressed up? You ain't tell me you were going somewhere."

"Girl, I'm going to meet Rich tonight at the Bone-Fish Grill."

Cashmere scowled. "Wheettt?! Since when you and Rich been hanging like that? Shit I thought it was over."

"It is over. I'm with Justin now and we're happy. He makes me feel good about myself. There is no drama or no other women and I love that about him."

"Yea, y'all are super cute together." Cashmere said. "So, but why are you meeting with Rich and dressed like that, I might add."

Fallin' In Love With The Goat 3

"We're meeting to settle this issue concerning the clubs. Yes, they are in my name and he wants them back once his divorce is final."

"Yea, I know so what have you decided to do?"

"Honestly, I don't know yet, but once I meet up with Rich and see what kind of attitude he has then I'll proceed. He has been laying low since Jabari jacked his ass up about a month ago. I bet after that, his ass ain't showed up to my house no more and the text messages stopped."

Cashmere bust out laughing. "Girrrrrl, if that shit ain't tickle me! I was so proud of Justin for laying hands on his ass. He was taking that stalking shit too fucking far."

"Well, when Justin wrapped them hands round that nigga's neck and slammed him on the ground. I think that shook his ass. Justin even took his gun from him and pointed it at his head. I honestly believe he shitted on himself. That's why he got the fuck outta there so fast."

Cashmere kept laughing. "Please Stop! That is some funny shit. I can see his red ass now trying to get somewhere."

"Girl, he was gettin' it too!" Shyla laughed out loud.

"Don't make me pee on myself." Cashmere said, while holding her stomach. "I wish you would've recorded it."

"Hell me too." Shyla mocked. "But, anyway he called all apologetic last night and asked that we meet up. I already know what it's about but I can never trust him fully. So, we'll see how that goes."

By: Tiece

"Well, make sure you have your mace on you just in case he gets outta pocket."

"Oh, don't worry. I got something for his ass." Shyla joked but was very serious. "Anyway, what's happening, Ms. Glow-Up? How are things with you and Ace?"

Cashmere blushed. "Ace and I are good, still getting to know one another. It's still so unbelievable to know that he and Jabari are brothers. Ain't that some shit?"

"Girrrrrl, it's a small fucking world. I know that." Shyla agreed. "Who would've ever known?"

"And honestly, he looks a lot like his mom, but he also looks just like a McCoy. I feel so out of place sometimes, just because he and Jabari are brothers. Like I've put my hoe days behind me. Sleeping with Slick was a mistake and the only good thing that'll come of that is if she's his," she said rubbing on her stomach. "But, I never wanted to cross Jabari like that again, whether we're together or not. But then, I meet Ace and we just click. Was I supposed to walk away from that feeling after I found out the truth?"

"Nope," Shyla said. "He didn't know, and you didn't either. Hell, he found out the same week they raced, but he didn't tell you until weeks later. That meant he didn't care."

"Yea, he said he wanted me to get to know him first before making a decision of cutting him off just because of the new revelations."

"I understand, but they didn't grow up together. I'm sure Jabari will understand."

"Yea, whenever I tell him." Cashmere uttered. "I just haven't said anything yet. I have so much going on with the baby coming, the baby shower is next week—"

"Yea, I know." Shyla said. "You ain't gotta tell me, but he's clearly moved on. I mean, I don't think he's in a relationship or nothing, but he hangs out with some lil red chick every now and then at the club."

"Yea, that's Cain's baby mama's sister. He told me that they're just good friends, but I think it's more brewing between the two. If nothing else, they're definitely fucking."

"I'm sure," Shyla concurred.

"Jabari is just living his life, and I can't blame him. I ain't mad at him. Regardless of what we went through in our relationship, he's still a good guy. Neither one of us are perfect and we both cheated, mine just a lil worse because of who it was with. But, we've gotten over it. We're friends, could be parents to this little one and if that's the case, then I'd like nothing more than for us to be cordial. I don't think he'd trip one way or the other about me talking to Ace. I mean, hell, we haven't even made it official. We're still learning each other. On top of that, we've not fucked yet."

"Oh, that'll happen soon and I mean soon as you have that 6 week check-up."

Cashmere laughed. "No, I'm serious."

"Bitch, me too, especially since he's moving here in a few weeks."

"Girl, I'm so excited about that." Cashmere blushed. "I just appreciate the fact that he accepts me, flaws and all. He didn't judge me when I told him about my situation. He's been nothing but kind-hearted and very chill about the whole thing. He really does have ways like Jabari. They're demeanors are so cool."

"Well, that's good bestie." Shyla said while glancing down at her watch. "On that note, I gotta go. Rich is probably pulling up at the restaurant now and my late ass ain't even left yet."

"Yea, well, call me when you make it back."

"You know I will." Shyla said, as she gave Cashmere a kiss on the cheek. "Love you."

"Love you too Bitch."

Cain walked to the door, as the light sound of knocking could be heard from the other side. He opened it up with a wide smile on his face. "Heyyy Daddy's big boy," he said, while reaching for Cannon.

Sofa handed him over. "Wassup Big head?" she said, as she followed him into his house.

"Same ole, same ole," Cain said, as walked through the kitchen then entered the living room. "Wassup with you?"

"Just going back home to get ready for this weekend. YoYo has something special planned at a cabin for my birthday. We're having a girl's weekend trip."

"Sounds like fun." Cain said, as he sat down on the couch. Cannon crawled out of his lap and took off in the direction called being nosy. As he looked for his something to get into, Sofia and Cain talked a little.

Fallin' In Love With The Goat 3

"So, how are you?" Sofia asked, as she looked around. It had been a couple of months since Lauren had left and still there was no sign showing that she was back.

"I'm good," he answered.

"You're back looking like the Cain I know." She teased. "I mean, a few weeks ago you were looking like a crackhead—"

Cain bust out laughing. "A crackhead? I wasn't looking that bad."

"Shittin' me!" Sofia laughed. "So, how's the bachelor life? Are you finally getting adjusted to it?"

"Yea, but I ain't trying to be out there like that."

"You ain't gotta be out there like that. Just get you a good cut-buddy, somebody like me." Sofia told him with a cute smile.

"Nah," Cain grinned. "I think we just need to co-parent. Nothing more or less," he added.

"I'm telling you. I don't talk. I won't be nothing like your other baby mama. She was crazy as hell for busting you out like that."

"Yea, I guess she had her reasons. I was pissed off about it at one point, but I'm over it now. She wasn't lying about nothing, I just hate the shit surfaced."

"Well, you know what they say. What happens in the dark comes to light."

Cain shrugged. "You're right." He said.

"Me and Hazel talked it out. We're cool, we have no choice but to be."

"Well, that's good." Sofia slid in.

"Do you think you and Lauren will get back together?"

"Nah, I doubt it, at least not right now." Cain said. "She's not playing with my ass."

"I guess, but she's crazy if you ask me. I mean, you took care of her. She didn't have to do nothing, but play the housewife. I would've done that in a heartbeat." Sofia said, as she called out to Cannon. "Put that down son." Then she continued. "I wouldn't have been complaining. Hell, men cheat all the time. That's just what y'all ugly asses do." she joked but was very serious. "She won't find another one to do the shit you did for her."

"Well, she's a good girl and she probably will. There are good men out there. It just takes a real man to know what he got and to hold on to her."

"I guess," Sofia said. "I still say she's crazy."

"Well, she's coming here in a lil bit to get some more of her stuff."

"She ain't got all of stuff yet? I think she's stalling for time. You better hurry up and make-up before she do find Mr. Right."

"Shit, at this point, ain't nothing I can do but lay low and chill. I ain't trying to pressure her or nothing like that. As long as she's back talking to me that's all that counts."

"Well, I'm about to go. You know me and her don't get along too well."

Cain laughed. "I know," he said, as Sofia stood to her feet. She wasted no time kissing Cannon and heading for the front door. "Thanks for keeping him for me."

"You know I don't mind." Cain said.

Fallin' In Love With The Goat 3

"I'm leaving just in time," Sofia said, as Lauren pulled up and parked.

Cain grinned with a shake of the head, as he watched the two pass each other. Both barely speaking.

"What she doing in here, fucking you?" Lauren teased.

Cain laughed. 'Well, hey to you too."

"Hey," she said with a playful smile. "Heyyy Cannon." she said leaning down to kiss him on the cheek. "You know I don't care for your baby mama's."

"I know," Cain responded.

"I'm not going to be long. I just got some clothes to get and then I'll be out of your hair."

"You don't have to rush off. We should be able to talk without the drama." Cain said, as Lauren continued her walk to the bedroom.

"I know, but I don't wanna be in the way. Plus, I just started back talking to you I don't want to regret it." She said.

"Damn, you've turned cold-hearted."

"You made me that way." Lauren told him.

Cain followed her in the bedroom, and put Cannon down on the floor to play. He looked over at Lauren. "You look beautiful."

"Thanks," she said. "You look good yourself."

"Preciate that." He told her. "Look, I know I've apologized over and over again, but I want you to know that I mean it."

By: Tiece

"I heard you every time you said it." Lauren said, as she grabbed a few things out of the drawer and began packing them inside the Coach duffle bag she had on her shoulder when she walked in.

"I hope you're doing more than just hearing me." Cain told her. "I miss you."

"I miss you too, but this ain't about me missing you. This is about me getting my life together and that's what I'm doing. I've enrolled back into school to become a professional Interior Decorator, along with other things that are closely related to that field."

"Well, that's good, but you could've been went to school. I never stopped you from doing that."

"I know you didn't, but I got comfortable with you taking care of me. I settled for that life. I lost everything about me along the way, but I'm back to being me and it feels good. I didn't realize how far off I had gone until I found myself."

"Well, I'm happy to hear that." Cain told her. It was almost nothing else he could do except be patient and pray that she'd one day come back around.

"That's all I needed to get." Lauren said, as she leaned down and kissed Cannon again. "See you later handsome."

"Let us walk you out." Cain said, as he picked Cannon up and walked Lauren to the door.

Lauren wasted no time walking out and heading to her car.

"Ayeee!" Cain called out. "Would go out on a date with me someday?" he asked just out of the blue.

Fallin' In Love With The Goat 3

Lauren stopped in her tracks and turned to look at him. "Maybe," she said with a smile. "See you later."

Cain smiled, as he watched her leave. There was hope for them yet and he wasn't going to give up on her.

Shyla sat across from Rich with a fake smile on her face. She couldn't believe she had allowed someone of his type to swindle her into thinking that he really loved her. He was bullshitter and a liar. She could never go back there with him again.

"You look beautiful this evening." Rich said, to start a lil small talk.

"Thanks," Shyla told him.

"You don't have to act so reserved. I'm sorry for the way I treated you." He said with a sincere look in his eyes.

"Apology accepted." Shyla said, as she looked over the menu.

"We're better than this."

"I know," Shyla said, as the waitress walked over.

"What can I get you?" she questioned them.

"I'll have 2 patron shots." Shyla said.

"They're ten-dollars a piece. I just have to let you know that when you order those, because people get their bills and be acting like they didn't know."

Shyla nodded her head. "I understand. Let me get 3 those instead."

"Okay," the woman said with a grin. "Sir, what can I get you?"

By: Tiece

"Uh, let me get some Hennessy with a splash of Sprite."

"Okay, I'll be back with those shortly. Did y'all want to order an appetizer?"

"No, thank you."

"No," Rich said, with a shake of the head.

"So, let's not prolong this outing. You wanted to discuss getting the clubs back?"

"Yea," Rich told her, as he opened the folder that was sitting on the table in front of him and pulled out some paperwork. He handed it to Shyla. She smirked while getting the paperwork. "Read over that and let me know what you think."

Shyla sat quietly as she read over the 1st page of the paperwork. She smugly grinned with a shake of the head, as she turned to the second page. It all seemed like a bunch of bullshit laid out on paper that wasn't really saying much of anything that she wanted to hear.

"So, the only thing it's saying is that within the next year, I will sign over the clubs back to you. I'll keep my manager pay, plus a raise of three dollars. So, that takes my monthly salary up to three-thousand a month?"

"Yea," Rich responded with a proud smile on his face.

The waitress walked back over with their drinks. "Here you go, 3 Patron shots, and here you go, Hennessy with a dash of sprite."

Shyla nodded her head, and then turned up one of her shots.

"Thanks," Rich told the waitress.

"Y'all ready to order." She asked.

"No, I think that'll be it for me." Shyla answered.

"Yea, me too." Rich commented.

"Okay," the waitress said, and then walked off.

"So, Rich, you want me to sign these papers within a year give you your clubs back?"

"Yea, is there a problem?"

"Yes, there is a big problem," Shyla responded. "I'm not signing these papers. However, I do have papers of mine that I need you to sign." She said while pulling her papers out.

Rich frowned. "What's this?"

"The papers that I need you to sign. Basically, it states that you're going to deposit four-hundred-fifty-thousand dollars into my bank account by tomorrow's date, plus four-thousand-dollars a month for the boys. I won't be returning back to work, so you can hire someone new. I quit as of last night." She told him.

"What?"

"Yes, Rich."

"Why is everything in 4's?" he asked with confused, irritated eyes.

"Because I dealt with your grimy ass four fucking years too long." Shyla shot his way. "You're not going to call the shots anymore. I am. Your wife told me about your finances and you think I was going to settle for that shit you have in those papers? Not at all. You're a millionaire, with businesses, property in different states, want me to keep going?" she questioned while throwing back her 2nd shot.

"No," Rich answered.

By: Tiece

"I expect you to sign these papers and have them back to my lawyer by tomorrow, and don't forget that deposit drop."

"Are you kidding me, Shy?"

"No, for once I'm so serious as hell. I'm not playing with you anymore. Either you do that or you won't get the clubs back. And, let's be honest here. They're worth way more than that." She mentioned. "So, what are you going to do?" she pondered.

"I'll deposit the money and I'll pay the four-thousand a month." Rich said in a defeated tone.

"Cool," Shyla said, while turning up her last shot.

Out of nowhere, Justin walked over. "You ready Babe?"

Shyla smiled at Rich and then she glanced upwards at Justin, as she stood up from her seat. "Yes Baby, we can leave now." And with that, she and Justin left Rich sitting at the table with a perplexed expression on his face. He'd lost at his own game and now he had to live with it.

As they made it out to the car, Shyla's cell phone rang. She answered it on the first ring.

"What's up, Bestie?"

"My water just broke!" Cashmere yelled in the phone.

"What?! it's not time for that."

"I knoooow, but your mom is taking me to the hospital now."

"Now?"

"Yes Now!" Cashmere exclaimed. "Okay, I'll meet you there."

Chapter Fourteen

Jabari awakened, sitting straight up in the bed. He stretched his arms out while yawning like he was still tired. However, he'd had a pretty laid back night of soft music, a relaxing full body massage, and some much needed rest. Nothing more or less but it was amazing to have spent such quality time with someone so on ice and patient with him.

It had been a month since baby Kari Alexis Lux was born and he'd been anxiously waiting to hear the results of the blood test. Because she was born early, they decided to wait until later to have the test done. There was no rush. It didn't matter to Jabari because he actually enjoyed being around the little one. He really couldn't tell who the father was, because Kari looked so much like Cashmere. However, just being in her presence was the sweetest thing ever.

Things had certainly changed; dynamics and all. Finding out that Ace was his brother seemed to have strengthened a family bond that they all shared. It was almost like they lost a sister but gained a brother in return. Even his mom was accepting of him, being that she and Biggs had split up during the time he was conceived. She even mentioned that there was a possibility that news of this kind could someday come to light. She just thought it would've been a lot sooner. Nevertheless, family was family and they were all each other had.

Even stranger was the fact that Cashmere and Ace were seeing each other. It wasn't confirmed that they were a couple, but since he had moved to Georgia, they seemed to have gotten a lot closer.

By: Tiece

At first, he was deep in his feelings when Cashmere explained to him that she and Ace were talking and that it was a possibility it could lead in a more serious direction. However, he couldn't hold that against her because none of them knew about Ace being a McCoy. It was pretty shocking to everybody involved. The only problem was that it would be weird for him to be Kari's father, knowing that her possible step-father was his brother.

He shook his head, trying to clear his thoughts. That had been something he struggled with since her birth. A part of him felt that she was his. It was hard enough knowing that he wasn't with her mother. But in a sense, he'd rather her talk to somebody that he knew would have her best interest at heart; especially Kari's.

Ace was indeed a good guy. He was a McCoy through and through. It was just unfortunate that they didn't know it early on being that they missed out on so much of each other's lives. However, there was no time like the present and they were definitely making up for it.

He placed his feet on the floor, sitting on the side of his bed. His cell phone rang, as he looked over at the time on his alarm clock. It was just after seven o'clock in the morning. The display of his phone showed that it was Cashmere calling. It could've only meant one thing, the test results were back. Quickly, he answered the phone.

"Wassup Cash?"

"Good morning Jabari," she said in her usual tone. "The results are back. I didn't open either of the emails because I wanted to read it with you on the phone."

"Okay," Jabari said, while literally sitting on the edge of his seat. "Just skip to the chase and read my results first."

"Okaaaay," Cashmere said, like she was now opening up the email. "Here goes."

Silence took over the call as he anxiously waited. "Well, what does it say?"

Cashmere cleared her throat. "Well, um, it says that you're not the father."

Jabari didn't say a word, as his heart skipped a beat. *Damn,* he thought. Something about hearing those words stung a little. He knew it was a possibility that she wasn't his, but during the past few weeks of her being here, he'd had a change of heart. "Wow," he let out. "So, I'm not her father?" he asked, but Cashmere didn't responded. "Read Slick's results please. I need to know if she's his baby."

Cashmere sniffed in the phone, he could tell that she'd started crying. "I'll just forward you both results." She told him. "I'll call you back." With that she quickly ended their call.

Jabari sat in silence, just as the results came through by text message. He opened the messages and went straight to Slick's DNA results. It showed that Kari was indeed his daughter. "Wow," he said again. It felt like a blow to his ego and his pride. He was hurt, but as he sat there, he started to calm down. Things happened for a reason. Maybe it wasn't meant for her to be his. Maybe it was meant for Slick to leave his legacy to a Princess. Maybe it was meant for him to see things that way. At that moment, he decided to call Cashmere back.

"Hello," she answered in a saddened tone.

"Hey it's me." Jabari said.

By: Tiece

"Hey you," Cashmere responded. "If you called to cuss me out I'm not in the mood."

"No, that's not why I'm calling at all. I really wanted to call and say that nobody what those test results say, I'm still going to be very active in Kari's life. Slick was my best friend, like a brother to me and I could never turn my back on his baby. I understand that we're both moving in different directions, but I think it was a reason for you and Ace linking."

"Why do you say that?"

"It takes a village to raise a baby, and we McCoy's don't back down from nothing or nobody. So, Kari will always be a light in our lives, more importantly, in Trudy's life as well. She'll always be good no matter what."

Cashmere cried on the phone, but it was that of happy tears. "Thank you so much Jabari. You don't know how much that means to me. Just to hear you say that has really given me so much hope for a lot of things, including loving again. Thank you."

"It's no problem." Jabari smiled. "Kiss Kari for me. Oh, don't forget that Ma wants to pick her up tomorrow. We're having this big family dinner thing she has planned. "

"I haven't forgotten and Thanks again Jabari. This call back really meant the world to me."

"A'ight, we'll talk later." Jabari said, and then ended their call. As he sat there he could feel a warm hand rubbing up and down his back.

"You okay?" a soft voice asked from behind.

Fallin' In Love With The Goat 3

Jabari smiled, as he turned to kiss Yolanda on the lips. "Yea, I've never been better." He responded.

"Let's shower." Yolanda said, as she sat up in bed.

Jabari frowned. "Me and you in the shower together? You know what's going to happen right?"

"Yea," she grinned with a seductive smile.

"Shit, I'm down." He grinned, while jumping out of bed. He felt good. Things were definitely moving in the right direction. Nothing could kill his vibe. However, just as he started to follow Yolanda in the bathroom, his cell phone alerted him of a text message.

The shop in an hour. BIGGS

Jabari knew that could only mean one thing. It was time to put an end to all the lies and betrayal that had been going on around them. Biggs and Papers had found out the truth and now it was time that they knew too.

He could hear the shower water running, as thoughts of filling up Yolanda crossed his mind. He walked to the bathroom door, while grabbing a pair of jeans off the chair to put them on. "Sorry Babe. I gotta make a quick run somewhere but I'll make it up when I get back."

"I think we should just leave town." Melissa said to Bruno.

"No, I have to go see what Biggs wants before we leave." Bruno responded, while driving the back country road.

"I have a bad feeling about this."

"Just calm down. They don't know anything."

"Yea, but for Biggs to bug your and our house meant something. If it wasn't for the hidden camera's we have around the house, we could've slipped up and said the wrong thing."

"Yea, but we knew and we didn't slip up and say nothing that would indicate my involvement in Slick's death or Skylar's."

Melissa shook her head with an irritated expression. "I should've stayed away. I don't know why I came back to you."

"You love me and you know deep down inside that you didn't want this to fall back on me because then it would fall back on you too."

"I wish I had never known about you getting that girl pregnant! She was too young for you anyway! What were you thinking?!"

"Melissa, we're not going back through this! Calm down!" Bruno yelled. He already had enough on his mind. The last thing he wanted was to bring that shit back up. It was the same thing he was trying to escape, which was the reason why he decided it was time for them to skip town. "I think we passed the test. We didn't say nothing out of the way. He even removed the bugs. So, we're good."

"But didn't you say that they were getting a paternity test done on that girl?"

"Yea, but he said that would take months, even years to come back. By then we'll be so far gone that they'll never locate us. Plus, it's a possibility the baby could've been Mar's. Just because she said it was mine didn't make it mine. She was fucking him too."

"I hear you." Melissa griped. "I just feel like for them to go through the lengths of trying to bug our house and your car that they're onto something. I mean, why else would they go through that?"

"Everybody close to them are suspect, that's all. However, I do believe we cleared ourselves. They heard the bugs I'm sure and they didn't hear nothing that implicated me."

"I don't understand why you're so cool about this." Melissa said. She wasn't seeing Biggs at all. She just wanted to get far away as possible. She was surprised to have stayed around that long. It was just strange for Biggs to know they were leaving town that day, so why wait till now to speak with Bruno?

Bruno pulled up to the gate and then punched in the code. "See, they haven't changed nothing." He said, as the gate opened.

"Why would they?"

"I'm just saying," Bruno uttered as he drove through the gate. He pulled up to the shop to see Justin standing outside flagging them down. He pulled up beside him.

"Wassup Bruno, hey Melissa."

"Hey Justin." Melissa spoke back with a fake smile.

"Nothing much," Bruno responded. "I just came by to meet up with your Pops before we head out."

"That's right, y'all leaving today."

"Yea, we're about to make a new start for ourselves. I think it's about that time."

Justin nodded his head. "I feel you. Well, Pops and the crew is in the warehouse out back. I just thought I'd let you know since I saw you pulling up."

By: Tiece

"Okay great." Bruno said, just as Melissa cut in.

"Do you know what he wanted to see Bruno about?"

"Uh, yea, I think he's giving him a gift for y'all leaving. Maybe some money," he added.

"Ohhh okay," Melissa said.

"Alright Justin. If I don't see you again, hold it down. Love ya Boy." He reached his hand out to shake Justin's hand.

"Safe travels." Justin said. Just hearing Bruno say he loved him ate at his core. He really wanted to punch the nigga and his wife.

"Thanks," Melissa smiled, as Bruno let his window up and pulled off.

"I told you it was nothing. I'm going to get this money and get the hell out of here."

"Good," Melissa said.

As Bruno entered the warehouse, everything seemed to be cool until Biggs' goons popped up out of nowhere. Two of them were holding a gun and pointing it in his direction. "What's going on?"

Biggs and Papers stepped out the back of the room, both with serious expressions on their faces.

"Biggs, Papers what's going on?" Bruno asked again with a scared look in his eyes.

"I think you should be telling us." Papers said, as he walked over and sucker-punched Bruno in the gut.

Bruno coughed while trying to catch his breath. "I don't know what you're talking about." He said through nervous breaths.

Fallin' In Love With The Goat 3

"Get on yo' knees!" Papers told him. "Playtime is over!"

"Why, what happened?" Bruno anxiously asked.

"Well, let's start from the night that my daughter was killed." Biggs said, as he kicked Bruno in the face with his steel toe boots on. Blood shot out his mouth, along with a tooth.

"Yea, let's talk about the secret relationship that you had with Skylar behind our backs." Papers said, as he bitch slapped him a few times to wake his ass back up. "Let's talk about all that!"

"What?! That's a lie!" Bruno yelled out, as the blood spilled from his mouth.

"No, it's not a lie!" Papers yelled back.

"See, Mars knew something that nobody else knew. However, he was afraid to come forward because it put him directly in the line of fire." Biggs said, while pulling out a bike camera that had all the horrid details of that night.

"What's that?!" Bruno frantically asked.

"Something that you should've made sure didn't exist." Papers told him.

"Well, let me break this shit down for you, since you're still acting innocent." Biggs told him. "Mars was a bike rider. He loved to record his speed along with the vision of seeing just how fast he could go. The night that Skylar was killed, he showed up to the warehouse first and hid his bike alongside the edge of the woods, but the camera on the bike continued to record."

"Fuuuuck," Bruno dragged in a scared tone.

By: Tiece

"What we witnessed was you go in to meet up with my baby girl. Clearly, a heated argument started, because eventually you came out looking pissed off and talking shit."

Bruno began to cry. "I'm sorry Biggs, it wasn't supposed to go down like that."

"Oh, now you wanna confess?" Papers cut in, as he rocked Bruno again across the face. "It's too late for that!"

"My daughter was alive when you came out of that warehouse, because eventually she emerged too. It looked like y'all had a few words and then you followed her back inside. What I wasn't expecting was Melissa pulling up."

Bruno started crying harder.

"Hush Bitch!" Papers told him. "Ain't no need to cry now!"

"Melissa got out the car with a gun in her hand. She went into that building and whatever happened, it happened quickly. See, we didn't have any sound inside the building, but outside the building was another thing. Melissa ran out of the building with you following her. Y'all were in panic mode. Not only was Melissa yelling at you for getting my daughter pregnant, but she kept saying it was all your fault. On top of that, Melissa was still holding the gun."

"Please, she had nothing to do with this!" Bruno yelled out, but caught another blow to the face by Papers.

"She had everything to do with this because she shot my baby and y'all left her for dead!" Biggs yelled out.

"She didn't mean too, the gun just went off."

"That's a lie!" Biggs shouted. "The gunshots were loud enough to hear from the bike cam, and she shot Skylar twice, once in the shoulder and the other in the stomach. That to me meant she was definitely aiming to kill the baby. After it was over, you didn't even check on my baby no more. You made Melissa get in her car and you followed her out of there, never looking back!"

"I didn't want her to die though!"

"But you didn't do anything to save her, either!" Biggs yelled, just as his goons walked Melissa through the warehouse doors.

"Brunoooo," she cried out.

"It's okay baby." Bruno said, with tears running down his face.

"Bitch you shut up too!" Papers intervened, and slapped Melissa so hard her wig flew off her head. "You didn't think we'd find out about you shooting my niece?! BITCH!" he yelled out, kicking Melissa to floor.

Melissa could barely hold her head up. She was still dazed from the slap she'd gotten. Finally, she looked at Bruno like she'd seen a ghost. "What's this? I told you we shouldn't have come here." She cried.

"Bitch, we would've found you!!" Papers yelled, "Get on yo' knees Hoe!"

"Papers," Biggs called out, to try and calm him down a little before it was too late. He had to finish his story, so that Bruno and Melissa felt his pain. "We've been sitting on this information for over a week. Just waiting for the right time to get the both of y'all here. That warehouse was the place my daughter died at, so I think it's the perfect place for y'all to die at too."

"Noooooooo," Melissa cried out.

"Biggs please, you don't have to do this." Bruno begged.

By: Tiece

"I know I don't! But see, I've been bothered by this whole ordeal."

"We didn't kill her Biggs," Melissa cried. "I didn't shoot her in the head!"

Biggs nodded his head to agree. "That's true. See, Mars entered the warehouse after y'all left. He found my baby fighting for her life. Instead of helping her, he got scared and left her there. His conscious apparently got to him and he returned a couple of hours later, only to find that she was still alive. He knew that if he let her live she would tell that he'd left her there to die. Just like the two of you did!" He angrily said, "And so he finished the job! Had it not been for his cousin giving me the bike cam we would never know what really happened," he explained. "He actually bought y'all some time because he wanted to give us the cam months ago. However, when he looked at it again, allowing it to play through to the end, he saw there was more. Mars returned only to finish the job. But your betrayal Bruno is something we didn't expect, you and your wife can count y'all minutes."

"On top of that, we found out that Slick confronted you about this and you killed him because he was onto you. The last you needed was for him to bring that shit to us."

"I didn't mean for any of that to happen! Slick was never supposed to die! He should've just stayed out of it!" Bruno cried.

"But it happened and he died because you couldn't handle him knowing the truth!" Papers yelled, just as two police officers rushed inside the warehouse.

"Bruno and Melissa Fields, you're both under arrest for the murder of Draymond 'Slick' Kelly, and for the murder of Skylar McCoy."

"Thank God," Melissa let out. She was happier to be going to jail than to get killed at the hands of Biggs and Papers."

The officers put cuffs on them, nodded at Biggs and Papers, and then walked out of the warehouse with Melissa and Bruno in tow. They put both of them in the back of the police car.

Biggs and Papers got in the truck together and followed the police car out.

As they passed back by the shop, the brothers were standing out front watching them with disheartened looks on their faces. Bruno couldn't even look their way, as he dropped his head from the shame of it all. Once the vehicles had disappeared, Jabari looked over at Justin and Cain.

"Damn, they actually think they're going to jail." He said, with a shake of the head.

"They're going to jail alright. I think it's called hell in Biggs and Papers world." Justin uttered.

"They gon' freak out when they see that they're being taken to the same warehouse that Skylar was killed in. I think it's only fitting that they leave the same way she did." Cain angrily stated.

Justin nodded his head. "I agree."

"We still didn't have solid evidence that he killed Slick, but I heard him admit it before I exited out the back doors. I know Pops had told us to leave because he didn't want us around for any of that, but I had to stay and hear if he was the grimy ass nigga behind that too."

"Well, you got your answer." Justin said.

"We all got our answers." Cain added.

"So, what now?" Justin pondered.

"We move on, leaving this moment behind us like it never happened." Cain answered.

"You're right Bruh. It's time to let it go and live the lives Slick and Skylar would've wanted for us." Justin said.

"Long live Skylar and Slick!" Jabari yelled out, with a satisfied smile on his face. "Sorry Boys, I got some ass to get back home to."

Cain and Justin laughed.

"Hell, me too." Justin nodded while thinking about Shyla.

"Well, I can get some ass but it ain't the ass I want. So, oh well, I'll pass."

Justin and Jabari laughed.

"You sound sad, my nigga." Jabari clowned.

"Go to hell." Cain grinned. "I'm calling Ace, he'll go to Club 1 with me."

"Yea, he's the life of the party," they laughed.

The brother's joked around a little longer before jumping in their cars and going their separate ways.

It may not have been the fairytale ending for some, but Bruno and Melissa had gotten exactly what was coming for them, and in the end, so did Mars.

Fallin' In Love With The Goat 3

The End...

By: Tiece

Other Books Written by Tiece...
*Falling In Love With The Goat 1-3 (Complete Series)
*Just Can't Leave Him Alone 1-5, Originally Titled, CheckMate (Complete Series)
*I Need Love 1-4, Originally Titled, SCARLETT (Complete Series)
*Drunk in Love 1-4 (Also Available In a Complete Box-set)
*Woman To Woman 1-3 (Also Available in a Complete box-set)
*The First Wife 1-3
*Shanice Capone's Truth, A Shorty Story (Located at the end of The First Wife part 3)
*Classy & Ratchet, Originally Titled, Ratchet Bitches 1-2
*Southern Gossip 1-2
*It's Either Me Or Her 1-2
*A Boss Valentine In Atlanta (A Short Story)
*These Games We Play 1
*Dopeboyz & the Women That Love 'em
*My Girl Got a Girlfriend 1-2 (Turned into A Standalone Novel)
*Shorty Found Love With a Dope Boy, Originally Titled, Thug Lovin' Is The Best Lovin' 1-2 (Turned into A Standalone Novel)

Fallin' In Love With The Goat 3

*For The Love Of My Trap King 1-2 Originally Titled, Shawty Is My Rock (A completed Series, Will be turned into a Standalone Novel)